CLUB
CSI:™

The Case of the Missing Moola

by David Lewman

Simon Spotlight

New York   London   Toronto   Sydney   New Delhi

This book is a work of fiction. Any references to historical events, real people, or real locales are used fictitiously. Other names, characters, places, and incidents are the product of the author's imagination, and any resemblance to actual events or locales or persons, living or dead, is entirely coincidental.

SIMON SPOTLIGHT

An imprint of Simon & Schuster Children's Publishing Division
1230 Avenue of the Americas, New York, New York 10020
© 2012 by CBS Broadcasting Inc. and Entertainment AB Funding LLC.
All Rights Reserved. CSI: CRIME SCENE INVESTIGATION in USA is a trademark of CBS Broadcasting Inc. and outside USA is a trademark of Entertainment AB Funding LLC.
All rights reserved, including the right of reproduction in whole or in part in any form. SIMON SPOTLIGHT and colophon are registered trademarks of Simon & Schuster, Inc. For information about special discounts for bulk purchases, please contact Simon & Schuster Special Sales at 1-866-506-1949 or business@simonandschuster.com.
Manufactured in the United States of America 0713 OFF
10 9 8 7 6 5 4 3
ISBN 978-1-4424-3395-3 (pbk)
ISBN 978-1-4424-4670-0 (hc)
ISBN 978-1-4424-6687-6 (eBook)
Library of Congress Control Number is available from the Library of Congress.

Cover illustration by Chris King
Design by Victor Joseph Ochoa

Chapter 1

For about the hundredth time, Corey counted the small stack of crumpled bills. "Forty-six . . . forty-seven . . . forty-eight," he muttered to himself. "Forty-eight dollars. Not bad. Just wish it was mine."

He could really use the money. With forty-eight dollars he could buy a video game, go to the batting cages, and still have some left to put toward that new electronic tablet he had his eye on, the Quark Pad. To buy one of those, he'd only have to save up for about . . . a million years.

He sighed. Unfortunately, even though he was holding all that cash right in his hands, it wasn't his. He stuck it in his pocket, so he'd stop staring at it. But he still kept thinking about it. "Forty-eight dollars . . ."

Corey closed his locker door and jogged to homeroom. He didn't want to be late. At Woodlands Junior High, Principal Inverno and all the teachers constantly stressed how important it was to be on time. And the basketball coach liked him to run as much as possible.

Besides, he really liked homeroom. His teacher, Mrs. Ramirez, was nice. And today was special. Not just an ordinary Monday toward the end of the school year.

As he hurried into the classroom, Jacob Ritter came up alongside him. Jacob was supercompetitive. From blowing bubble-gum bubbles to throwing free throws, Jacob always wanted to be the best. "So," he asked, "what's your final total?"

Smiling proudly, Corey answered, "Forty-eight."

Jacob snorted and shook his head. "Too bad."

"Too bad?" Corey asked. "I thought forty-eight was pretty good."

"I guess," Jacob said, shrugging. He slung his backpack off his shoulder and slid slowly into a seat. His bag hit the floor. *Thump*.

"Why?" Corey asked, sitting down next to him. "How much did you raise?"

Jacob grinned. Clearly, this was exactly the question he'd wanted Corey to ask him. He leaned back in his seat and put his hands behind his head. "My final total was a hundred and forty-four."

"A hundred and forty-four bucks?!" Corey exclaimed.

"That's right," Jacob said, nodding slowly. "A hundred and forty-four dollah, dollah bills, y'all. I'll bet that's the most anyone collected!"

"Well, that's . . . really good," Corey admitted. He wished he could say something funny to take Jacob down a notch or two, but he couldn't think of anything offhand. If only his best friends, Ben and Hannah, were there. He always felt more clever when they were around.

The three friends had known one another since they'd entered kindergarten in their small Nevada town, but in seventh grade they'd ended up in separate homerooms. Luckily, they still had several classes together, including their favorite, forensic science with Miss Hodges. They liked that class so much, they'd even started their own extracurricular organization, Club CSI.

Corey was proud that as a member of Club CSI, he'd helped solve the mystery of why the cafeteria's meatless meat loaf had made several people sick. The principal of the school had even congratulated Club CSI on a job well done. If Corey helped solve more crimes, he thought, maybe someday the mayor would shake his hand and give him a medal. Or even the president . . .

The bell then rang, ending Corey's daydream. Mrs. Ramirez, a short woman with brown hair and glasses, got right down to business. "Good morning, class," she said cheerfully. "Today we're going to start by finding out how much you've all collected from selling magazine subscriptions."

A small cheer went up among the students. They knew Mrs. Ramirez would let them goof around a little in homeroom. But just a little.

"I'm hoping, as I'm sure you all are, that you've brought in enough money to pay this class's share of our trip to Washington, DC," Mrs. Ramirez said, smiling. "All right. Please bring up your money to me one at a time."

A black-haired girl named Jean popped up out of her seat in the first row and hurried up to Mrs. Ramirez's desk. Jean liked to be first. She was big on getting things over with.

"Here's mine, Mrs. Ramirez," she said a little nervously. "I really tried to sell as many subscriptions as I could." She handed a slim stack of bills to the teacher.

As Mrs. Ramirez thumbed the bills onto her desk one by one, she counted out loud. "Thirty-five, thirty-six, thirty-seven. Thirty-seven dollars. Good job, Jean."

Jean grinned, relieved. She'd worried that she hadn't sold enough magazine subscriptions. It wasn't easy. Nowadays it seemed as though everybody just read magazine articles online for free.

"Who can tell me something interesting about the number thirty-seven?" Mrs. Ramirez asked the class. Mrs. Ramirez was a math teacher, and she never missed a chance to mix a little math into her homeroom class.

Everyone looked stumped. Corey raised his hand tentatively. "It used to be Ron Artest's number?"

Now it was Mrs. Ramirez's turn to look stumped. "And who, exactly, is Ron Artest?"

"A basketball player," Corey explained. "For the Lakers."

"Except now he wants people to call him Metta World Peace," another boy, Victor, added.

"I will never get used to that," Corey said. "It'd be really hard to go to a game and yell, 'Go, Metta World Peace!'"

"What have you got against world peace?" Victor asked, grinning.

Mrs. Ramirez felt they were seriously getting off the topic at hand. "Thirty-seven," she announced, "is a prime number. Which means . . . ?"

"A number bigger than one that can be evenly divided only by one and itself," answered Emma Welch. She was really good at math.

"That's right!" said Mrs. Ramirez. "Next?"

A kid named Lukas gave Mrs. Ramirez the money he'd collected. Again, she counted it out loud, announcing the total: "Fifty-four dollars. Quick, is fifty-four divisible by three?"

"Yes," several kids said.

"How do you know?" Mrs. Ramirez asked.

Corey actually knew this one. He raised his hand, and Mrs. Ramirez called on him. "Because five plus four equals nine, and nine is divisible by three, so fifty-four is too," he explained.

"Very good!" Mrs. Ramirez said. Corey couldn't help but look proud.

The next student brought up twenty-eight dollars. "And what's special about the number twenty-eight?" the homeroom teacher asked.

The students thought about the number twenty-eight. Divisible by four. Divisible by seven. And two. And fourteen. But was that special?

"My birthday is on the twenty-eighth!" said Mrs. Ramirez, laughing. "So I'm always happy when I see the number twenty-eight!"

After Mrs. Ramirez counted each student's money, she wrote the amount on an envelope, along with the day's date. Then she put the money in the envelope and handed it back to the student. She also wrote each student's total on a separate piece of paper so she could add it up at the end. She liked her students to see her doing math by hand instead of using a calculator.

Each student would then open the metal box on Mrs. Ramirez's desk and place his or her envelope in the box. The money in the box would be kept safe by a combination padlock.

Jacob held back until all the other students had turned in their money. He was pretty sure he'd sold the most magazine subscriptions, and he wanted his contribution to be the triumphant finale. Each time Mrs. Ramirez announced a student's total, Jacob listened carefully to make sure it wasn't higher than his. And in every case, it wasn't. Sweet. The morning was going exactly as Jacob had imagined it.

"Is that everyone?" Mrs. Ramirez asked.

"No, Mrs. Ramirez," Jacob said, getting to his feet. "I've still got mine."

He strolled to her desk, savoring the moment. As she counted the fat pile of bills, the other students murmured in appreciation at the impressive total. "One hundred and forty-four dollars! Very well done, Jacob!" Mrs. Ramirez said. "That's the highest total yet!"

Jacob smiled and nodded. "Well," he said, "it's not so tough when you're a highly skilled salesman."

Mrs. Ramirez handed Jacob his envelope. As he was putting it in the metal box, she asked, "Can you tell me the square root of one hundred and forty-four?"

Jacob frowned. "The square root? Um, let's see . . ."

"Twelve!" Emma quickly blurted out. She knew Mrs. Ramirez was asking Jacob, but she just couldn't help herself.

"I was asking Jacob, Emma, but yes, twelve

is the square root of one hundred and forty-four," Mrs. Ramirez said. "One hundred and forty-four is also known as a gross—twelve times twelve."

"Jacob's total is gross," Victor said. The class laughed.

Corey wished he'd said that.

"So," Mrs. Ramirez said, adding up columns of numbers and writing with a pencil, "that brings our grand total to . . . one thousand two hundred and eighty-six dollars! Just two hundred and fourteen dollars short of our fifteen-hundred-dollar goal!"

Everyone cheered. "Washington, here we come!" Jean said.

"I'm sure we'll be able to raise the rest of the money with our bake sale in two weeks," Mrs. Ramirez added. She closed the padlock on the metal box, put the box in her desk drawer, and locked the drawer.

"Wow, one thousand two hundred and eighty-six dollars," Corey murmured. "With that much money, I could buy *two* Quark Pads. . . ."

"Dream on," Victor said.

"Thanks," Corey answered. "I will."

Chapter 2

On Thursday, Corey was back in homeroom. So far, it hadn't exactly been the greatest week of the school year for him. On Tuesday he'd forgotten to bring his science homework. On Wednesday he'd been caught off guard by a question because he was staring out the window during history class.

It was hard to concentrate this close to the end of the school year. Sometimes it felt like there was a choir outside singing, *"Summer, summer, summer . . ."*

But today he was going to focus. He was going to pay attention, no matter how tempting it was to look out the window and think about baseball. Or basketball. Or his family's summer trip to a lake in the mountains. Maybe this year he'd get up the nerve to dive off the high rock into that icy cold lake water—

Focus!

He forced his eyes away from the window and stared straight ahead. At the front of the classroom, Mrs. Ramirez was looking through her attendance sheet. The bell rang, and she looked up.

"Good morning, class," she said.

"Good morning," the students repeated, though it sounded more like a drone than a hearty greeting. Maybe they all had spring fever.

Mrs. Ramirez took attendance and then used a remote to switch on the TV mounted on a bracket near the ceiling. "All right," she said. "Let's all pay close attention to the morning announcements."

"Good morning, Woodlands Junior High School," said the girl on the TV screen. Corey thought she was an eighth grader. Most of the kids who got to be on the morning announcements program were eighth graders. Sometimes he thought being on TV might be fun, though he'd rather appear as a professional basketball player. A player who would never change his name.

The announcements were pretty standard—about

where to pick up yearbooks, birthdays, and what delicious items would be featured in the cafeteria at lunchtime. Corey kind of wished they wouldn't talk about lunch. Any mention of food made Corey hungry. And lunch period was still hours away.

After the morning announcements were done, Mrs. Ramirez turned off the TV and said, "I see that Bill is back with us today." Bill Hamm had been absent for the first half of the week.

"How was the big family reunion, Bill?" the teacher asked.

"Good," Bill said. He didn't much like talking in front of the whole class. But he did have something he was looking forward to sharing. Something . . . impressive.

And he was going to get his chance right away. "Did you happen to bring in the money you collected from selling magazines?" Mrs. Ramirez asked.

"Yep," Bill said. Then he smiled, a wide, proud grin.

"Well, then, please bring it up to the front," Mrs. Ramirez said.

Bill stood up. He was tall and lanky, and everyone watched as he walked to the front of the classroom.

He certainly looked pleased with himself.

Corey whispered to Jacob, "Uh-oh. Do you think Bill might have shattered your unbreakable record?"

"No way," Jacob shot back. But he looked worried, like he was holding his breath.

Bill pulled a stack of bills out of his back pocket. Jacob exhaled, relieved. The stack seemed smaller than the one he had brought in on Monday. Still, could it all be big bills instead of singles?

Then Bill pulled another stack out of his other back pocket. Corey whistled. Jacob groaned.

Mrs. Ramirez took the two stacks of cash, combined them, and started counting. The whole class leaned forward in their seats, listening, waiting to hear what the total would be.

When she said, "One hundred and fifty," Jacob slumped in his seat.

"That," Corey said, "is the sound of a record shattering."

But Mrs. Ramirez wasn't done counting. She kept going until she reached the last bill. She put it on the stack on her desk and said, "Two hundred and sixteen dollars! We've reached our goal! In fact, we're two dollars over!"

The class cheered. Bill smiled, looking embarrassed. Mrs. Ramirez handed him an envelope with his total written on it. As he put the money in the envelope, she asked him how he managed to raise so much money.

Bill shrugged. "I have a lot of relatives," he said.

Mrs. Ramirez addressed the class. "Should we double-check our math to make sure we've reached our fifteen-hundred-dollar goal for the trip to Washington?"

"Yes!" they shouted. The students had managed to shake off their spring fever, and were excited about their grand total.

Mrs. Ramirez took a key out of her pocket and unlocked her desk drawer. She lifted up the metal box and set it on her desk. She quickly spun the dial on the combination padlock, removed the lock, and pulled the lid open. *Click.*

Mrs. Ramirez offered the metal box to Bill. He picked up the box and added his bulging envelope to the others.

Mrs. Ramirez gave Bill a little nod of appreciation. He handed the box back to her. She took all the envelopes out one by one, opened them, and counted the money inside. But when she finished,

instead of one thousand five hundred and two dollars, she came up with a total of one thousand four hundred and two dollars. A hundred dollars short!

Could she have counted wrong?

As the class watched, Mrs. Ramirez carefully counted the money again.

One thousand four hundred and two dollars.

She didn't think she could possibly have made a mistake. And as she checked each student's envelope, she realized Jacob's envelope held only forty-four dollars.

"But there was definitely a hundred and forty-four dollars in there!" Jacob protested. "It was the most anyone collected!"

"Until Bill," Emma pointed out.

"Yeah . . . ," Jacob admitted, "until Bill. But on Monday my envelope had the most money in it. A hundred and forty-four dollars! Everyone knew that!"

"Right," Victor said. "Because you kept telling us."

It seemed clear that someone had stolen one hundred dollars from Jacob's envelope. Everyone in the homeroom started whispering to one another. Who could have taken the money?

Wasn't the box locked? And the desk? Only Mrs. Ramirez had the key. Did she take the money herself? She was driving a new car, but you can't buy a new car with a hundred dollars. And besides, she'd started driving the new car before Monday. Whoever stole the money must have taken it after Monday.

Another student thought maybe a janitor might have taken it. The janitors came in at night, after everyone left, so they'd have plenty of time to open the desk and the padlock to take the money. Another student said that kind of thinking was totally unfair to janitors. Janitors were people, too.

An international gang of thieves? That seemed pretty unlikely. They probably would have taken all the money.

Mrs. Ramirez called for everyone's attention. "Class, please. Let's stop all this talking. This is a classroom, not a coffee shop."

Jean raised her hand. "Does this mean the trip to Washington is canceled?"

Mrs. Ramirez shook her head. "No. We still have the bake sale. And perhaps whoever took the money will return it. That would certainly be the right thing to do."

That seemed kind of doubtful to Corey. Why would you go to all the trouble to steal a hundred dollars and then just give it back?

But that wasn't all Corey was thinking about. Before Mrs. Ramirez quieted everyone down, Corey was pretty sure he'd heard Victor saying something to a couple of kids about "a Quark Pad." And then he'd looked right at Corey. Suspiciously.

Were people thinking that he'd taken the money? No matter how much he'd like to have one of the new Quark Pads, he'd never steal money to get one. He had a strong urge to jump to his feet and yell, "I didn't do it!"

But that would probably make people suspect him even more.

Corey needed to clear his name. And he knew just the two people who could help him do it. . . .

Chapter 3

It smelled really good in the cafeteria at lunchtime that day. Mrs. Collins had fixed her special lasagna, which was one of Corey's favorites. But instead of devouring it, he just pushed at a piece with his fork.

"Okay," Hannah said. "What's wrong?"

"Yeah," Ben chimed in. "In a normal world, that lasagna would be at least halfway gone by now. In fact, make that three-quarters gone. Are you feeling sick?"

When you've known one another since kindergarten, your friends can instantly tell when you're not acting like yourself. And Corey was not acting like the Corey who Ben and Hannah knew.

"No," Corey said. "I'm not sick. But I'm worried.

Did you hear about what happened in Mrs. Ramirez's homeroom this morning?"

"You mean the missing money?" Ben said. "Of course we heard about it."

"News travels fast in this school," Hannah said, cutting off a piece of lasagna with her fork. "Why are you worried about it? Did you take it?"

"No!" Corey said, almost jumping to his feet. "Of course not!"

Hannah held up her nonfork hand. "Okay, I know! I'm just kidding!" She popped a bite of lasagna into her mouth and chewed. She'd chosen the vegetarian lasagna, and it was really good. Ever since Miss Hodges had complained that there weren't enough healthy choices being offered in the school cafeteria, Mrs. Collins had been trying to include more vegetarian food and other healthy options.

Corey looked glum. "Well, it's not funny. I think some people think I stole that hundred bucks, just because I was talking about how I wished I had enough money to buy one of those new Quark Pads."

"Those are so cool," Hannah said.

"You mean like the one Jeff Williams is using over there?" Ben asked, pointing with his fork.

Corey twisted in his seat to see where Ben was pointing. Sure enough, Jeff was showing off his Quark Pad to several admiring kids. A video played across the screen of the sleek electronic device. Bass music thumped from its tiny speaker.

"Man! How did Jeff get one of those? They're really expensive," Corey said.

"I'm not sure," Hannah said. "Maybe his parents bought it for him. I've been seeing more and more kids using them."

"Why don't people suspect Jeff of taking the money?" Ben asked.

"He's not in Mrs. Ramirez's homeroom," Corey said.

"Does it really have to be someone in her room?" Hannah asked.

"I don't know," Corey said. "I just know that it seemed like Victor was telling people I did it."

Ben thought for a minute. "So, what do you want us to do? Mount some kind of publicity campaign?" He moved his hand across an imaginary banner. "'Corey—In Your Hearts, You Know He's Innocent,'" Ben said dramatically.

"Maybe you're overreacting," Hannah remarked. "Do people really think you're the thief?"

"I'm not sure," Corey admitted. "But they might. And I hate that."

"We need more evidence," Hannah said.

"I've got an idea," Ben said. "We'll split up and walk around the cafeteria, trying to hear what people are talking about."

"Won't people notice me wandering around the room, eavesdropping?" Corey asked. "They'll shut up right away."

"Pretend you're getting more food or something," Hannah suggested. "Even if they don't say anything around you, you'll notice if they suddenly shut up. And maybe Ben or I will hear something."

"Okay," Corey said with a sigh. "I guess it's worth a try."

The three friends got up and went in three different directions. They made their way past as many tables as possible, trying to overhear what people were talking about.

It wasn't easy. The cafeteria was a pretty noisy place. Still, it became clear right away that lots of people were talking about the stolen money.

After a few minutes, Ben, Hannah, and Corey met back at their table to compare notes and finish their lunches before the bell rang.

"Well?" Corey asked. "Did you find out anything?"

Hannah nodded. "Definitely."

"What?" Corey asked anxiously.

"Well," Hannah said, leaning in and lowering her voice, "Sarah Clark has a huge crush on Zach Phillips."

"That's not what I meant!" Corey said.

"Yeah, Hannah," Ben agreed. "Everybody knows Sarah has a crush on Zach." He grinned.

"Fine," Corey said. "Just keep teasing me. Meanwhile, I'm getting a reputation as a no-good, lousy crook."

"That's not true," Ben said. "You took a hundred dollars. You're a very good crook."

Corey threw up his hands and laid his head on the table, moaning.

"Okay, okay," Hannah said with a laugh. "Enough teasing. I didn't hear anyone say that they thought you took the money. But lots of people are talking about the theft."

Ben nodded. "That's what I heard too. Everyone's talking about it. Except Mike Crowley. He's talking about—"

"Don't tell me," Corey interrupted. "Fly-fishing."

Ben looked surprised. "That's right. How did you know that?"

Corey rolled his eyes. "Ever since Mike's uncle took him on a fly-fishing trip, it's all he ever talks about. Wading into streams, casting, making your own flies, different kinds of trout—he won't talk about anything else."

Hannah made a face. "Fishing is gross. Blech."

"Unless you're starving on a deserted island and the only thing to eat is fish," Ben said.

"Still gross," Hannah insisted. "Just necessary, I guess."

"So, anyway, you didn't hear anyone talking about me being the thief?" Corey asked.

Hannah and Ben shook their heads.

"I guess that's good," Corey said. "But it doesn't really prove that no one suspects me. It just means you didn't happen to overhear them saying it."

Ben nodded. "That's true. I can only think of one sure way to prove that you didn't steal that hundred dollars."

"How?" Corey asked. "Search my room? Because you should know, it's a mess. And there's a missing sandwich. Might be pretty moldy by now."

"No," Ben said. "By finding out who *did* steal the money."

Hannah smiled. "That's a great idea! This could be Club CSI's second case."

"The Case of the Missing Moola," Ben said.

For the first time that lunch period, Corey brightened up. "Yeah! We could investigate, crack the case, find the real thief, and clear my name!"

"Using forensic science," Ben added.

"Naturally," Corey said. "That's the Club CSI way."

"What's our first step?" Hannah asked. "Search Corey's room?"

Corey frowned. "I thought we agreed no more teasing."

"Okay, sorry," Hannah said, giggling.

"I suggest," Ben said, "that we begin by consulting with our faculty advisor, Miss Hodges."

"Agreed," Hannah said.

"Boy, I feel better already," Corey said. "And hungry!"

Just as he started to tuck into his lasagna, the bell rang. *Brrrrrring!*

Chapter 4

At the end of the day, Hannah, Corey, and Ben managed to squeeze into Miss Hodges's small office off her forensic science classroom. The walls had posters about footprints, tire treads, and blood types. Her desk was covered with books and papers, neatly arranged into piles.

"All right, Club CSI," Miss Hodges said, smiling. "What's on your minds?"

"Theft," Ben answered.

"What's been stolen?" she asked, cocking her head to the side.

They explained about the money missing from Mrs. Ramirez's metal box. Miss Hodges listened carefully, nodding.

"I see," she said. "Well, I think in a case like this,

the first thing to determine is whether there actually has been a crime committed."

The three friends looked puzzled. How could robbery not be a crime?

"What I mean is," Miss Hodges explained, "are you absolutely sure Mrs. Ramirez didn't accidentally miscount the money?"

Ben and Hannah turned to Corey, since he was the one who was there when the money was counted. He thought a minute.

"I don't think she did," he said slowly. "For one thing, she's a math teacher."

"Yes, but even teachers can make some mistakes," Miss Hodges said. "I've made one or two myself."

"But the whole class was watching while she counted the money," Corey said. "And she counted it twice. The total was short a hundred dollars. When she checked Jacob's envelope, it was missing a hundred dollars."

Miss Hodges nodded. "All right, good," she said. "You're remembering the whole incident very clearly. And it sounds as though there wasn't a miscount. But could the hundred dollars have been lost somehow?"

Corey shook his head. "I don't really see how. Mrs. Ramirez put each person's money into envelopes, then locked the envelopes in a metal box. Right away."

"And then she locked the metal box in her desk drawer, right?" Ben added, since Corey had already told them every detail of the theft.

"Right," Corey said. "And the money was missing from Jacob's envelope. It had the most money in it."

"Since Jacob made a point of turning his money in last," Hannah added, "his envelope was right on top."

"Yeah, everyone in the class knew that," Corey said. "Whoever took the money probably just grabbed it out of Jacob's envelope because it was the fattest one."

"And the handiest one," Ben said, "sitting right there on top of the stack."

Miss Hodges had jotted down a few notes: "$100," "locked box," "Jacob," "top envelope." "Okay," she said. "From what you're telling me, it does sound quite likely that a theft actually has occurred. The money wasn't miscounted or misplaced. We'll go on the assumption that it was stolen."

All three kids nodded in agreement. They were sure the money had been stolen. And they were glad Miss Hodges agreed with them.

"So what's your first step?" Miss Hodges asked.

"Coming to you for advice," Corey answered.

Miss Hodges laughed. "Right," she said. "Well, I think I would suggest that you begin by putting together a timeline."

Corey was confused. "A timeline? Like we do in history class? Like, with the year Magellan sailed and the year Columbus reached the New World? We should get some high-quality poster board, because that's how I got an A on my explorers report in fourth grade."

Miss Hodges smiled. "I don't think we'll need poster board, though that's a great idea if you're making a presentation."

"I prefer PowerPoint," Ben said. He liked using his computer every chance he got.

Miss Hodges stood up. "Come on," she said. "Let's go in the lab. It's a little crowded in my office."

Hannah loved it when Miss Hodges called the forensics classroom "the lab." It sounded so official. Hannah was thinking about becoming a crime-scene investigator someday and was looking forward to working in a real police lab.

Ben, Corey, and Hannah followed Miss Hodges into the lab. There were tables and chairs, drawers and microscopes, but the teacher walked straight to the dry-erase board and picked up a marker.

"I think I know what kind of timeline you have in mind," Ben said. He turned to Corey. "When did Mrs. Ramirez put Jacob's envelope, with one hundred and forty-four dollars in it, in the metal box?"

"First thing Monday morning," Corey answered, "during homeroom period."

Miss Hodges handed the marker to Hannah. She pulled off the cap and wrote on the board "Monday morning—money put in box." As she wrote, the smell from the marker filled the air.

"When did Mrs. Ramirez discover that a hundred dollars was missing?" Ben asked.

"Thursday morning—today," Corey said. "Right after the morning announcements."

Hannah then wrote on the board: "Tuesday," "Wednesday," and "Thursday." Under "Thursday" she wrote, "After announcements, $100 missing."

"Did the metal box leave her desk drawer between Monday and Thursday?" Ben asked.

"Yes," Corey said confidently.

"When?" Hannah asked, ready to write this on the board.

"When the thief took the money," Corey said.

Miss Hodges grinned. "Corey, your logic is impeccable."

"I'm sorry," Corey said.

"Impeccable logic is good," Ben said.

"Why, because it can't be pecked?" Corey asked. "I'm confused."

Strolling toward the timeline, Miss Hodges explained, "All I'm saying is that you're right. The thief must have taken the box out of the desk. Between Monday morning and Thursday morning, did you see anyone take the box out of the drawer? Mrs. Ramirez, for example?"

"You're not saying Mrs. Ramirez stole the money, are you?" Corey asked, alarmed. "Because I'm pretty positive she didn't."

"I'm just trying to track the metal box, figure out where it was the whole time," Miss Hodges said.

Corey thought a minute. "Nope," he said. "I

don't think Mrs. Ramirez took the box out of the drawer. Unless she took it out for just a second while I was looking out the window or something. I've been looking out the window a lot lately."

"Spring will do that to you," Miss Hodges said, grinning. "But try to stay focused."

"I am," Corey said. "So, what does the timeline tell us?"

They all stared at the board. "Obviously," Hannah said, "the timeline suggests that the money was stolen between Monday morning and Thursday morning."

"Who had access to Mrs. Ramirez's classroom during that time?" Miss Hodges asked.

"All the students in her classes," Corey said.

"But it probably wasn't taken during a class, while she was right there," Ben said.

"Still," Hannah said, "classrooms aren't locked during the day. Anyone inside the school could slip in for a minute while the room was empty. Even teachers have to go to the bathroom."

Then she remembered she was talking to a teacher and felt a little embarrassed.

"So you're saying pretty much everyone in the school had access to that room," Ben said.

"Right," agreed Hannah, happy to leave the subject of teachers and bathrooms.

Corey whistled. "That's a big list of suspects." He wasn't exactly sure how many kids went to Woodlands Junior High, but he was pretty sure it was in the hundreds.

Miss Hodges nodded. "Clearly, you're going to need to gather some evidence."

"What kind of evidence?" Corey asked.

"Well, I think you might find tomorrow's class very informative," Miss Hodges said mysteriously. "And helpful."

"Why?" Hannah asked. "What are we learning about in forensic science tomorrow?"

Miss Hodges smiled and raised one eyebrow. "Wait and see."

As the three friends walked through the empty halls to their lockers before heading home, they talked about what tomorrow's forensic lesson might be.

"Whatever it is, I hope it helps us solve this case," Hannah said.

When he reached his locker, Corey found a piece

of notebook paper taped to the door. Someone had scrawled "I KNOW YOU STOLE IT!" on the paper. Corey ripped the paper off his locker and wadded it up.

"Yeah," he said. "The sooner the better."

Chapter 5

The next day Ben, Corey, and Hannah got to forensic science class early. They were eager to find out what Miss Hodges was going to teach them. Maybe it would help them figure out who stole the hundred dollars.

As he looked around class, Corey couldn't help but feel jealous when he noticed two or three kids using Quark Pads. *Maybe I should ask for a raise in my allowance,* he thought. *Or get a job. One that pays a ton of money. . . .*

Once everyone was seated and the bell had rung, Miss Hodges said, "All right. I'd like each of you to look at your left hand. What do you see?"

One kid said, "Jelly," and got a laugh. Another said, "Dirt." More laughter.

"Maybe I should have had you wash your hands first," Miss Hodges said. "Look past anything messy that's stuck to your hand. Pick just one finger and look very closely at the top section, above the joint. Now what do you see?"

All the students stared at their fingers.

"Little lines?" Kaylee said.

"Fingerprints!" Ricky Collins said. His mom was in charge of the cafeteria at Woodlands Junior High. She'd often complained about having to clean the kids' greasy fingerprints off her clean counters.

"Fingerprints are what we're going to study today," Miss Hodges said. The class murmured, excited. "But fingerprints are what your fingers leave behind. Your fingers don't have fingerprints on them, just like your feet don't have footprints on them. Does anyone know what those little lines on your fingers are called?"

No one knew. Not even Ben, who often knew all the answers. It was strange to think that for years they'd known they had lines on their fingers, but they'd never even thought about what the lines were called.

"They are called friction ridges," Miss Hodges

explained as she wrote the phrase on the board. "They help our hands grasp things, the same way ridges and grooves on a tire help it grip the road. All humans have them, and everyone's friction ridges are unique. Even identical twins have different friction ridges."

Tossing the marker in the air and catching it, she asked, "Do any other animals have friction ridges on their fingers?"

Hannah raised her hand. "I think I read somewhere that koala bears have fingerprints that look a lot like human fingerprints."

"That's right, Hannah," Miss Hodges said. "Very good! Koala fingerprints look so much like human fingerprints that it's actually hard to tell them apart."

"I love koalas," Hannah added.

"Other great apes, like gorillas and orangutans, also leave fingerprints," Miss Hodges continued. "And there are even some monkeys in South America that can leave prints with the pads on their tails. Their tails have pads with friction ridges, so they can use their tails to hang on to branches in the rainforest."

She went on to talk about the history of using

fingerprints to identify criminals. "Although people have known about fingerprints for a very long time, it was in the eighteen hundreds when they started to get the idea of using fingerprints to catch crooks," Miss Hodges said.

She told the class about Sir William Herschel, an Englishman in India who kept records of his own prints for over fifty years and noticed that they didn't change.

Miss Hodges talked about Henry Faulds, a doctor in Japan who wrote in 1880 about using fingerprints to identify criminals, and about Sir Francis Galton, who, in 1892, wrote the first book about fingerprints.

Ricky asked if all of this was going to be on a test. "Yes," Miss Hodges said. Everyone started to take more notes.

After reviewing the history of fingerprinting, Miss Hodges told the class how fingerprints are analyzed by experts. She passed around magnifying glasses, asking the students to look for loops, arches, and whorls (kind of like tiny whirlpools) in their fingerprints. Experts use these features to put fingerprints in different categories. She told them the FBI has a huge database of fingerprints in a computer called IAFIS, for Integrated Automated Fingerprint Identification System.

Ben quickly found a whorl in the middle of his right index finger. Soon all the students were comparing arches, loops, and whorls. But the really interesting part was when Miss Hodges showed the class how to lift a print from a crime scene.

She had students run their fingers through their hair and then touch different surfaces—glass, marble, shiny painted wood. "Your fingers have pores that produce oil, so you can leave fingerprints without touching your hair, but doing it this way, we'll be sure," she explained.

"Especially you, dude," one of Ricky's friends said to him. For that he got a quick punch in the arm. Luckily for Ricky, Miss Hodges didn't notice.

After they'd touched the surfaces, Miss Hodges had the students check them for fingerprints. Some they could see clearly. Others they could see more easily if they used a bright light.

"To help them see fingerprints," Miss Hodges said, "investigators use special powders like these." She brought out small jars of black, gray, and white

powder. If the surface was light-colored, they used black or gray powder. If the surface was dark, they used white.

The students took turns using small makeup brushes to carefully apply powder to the fingerprints. "Don't use too much powder," she cautioned, "or you'll cover up the print. And remember to brush very lightly, or you'll smear the print."

That's exactly what happened the first time Corey tried powdering one of his fingerprints. But soon he got the hang of lightly dusting a small amount of powder onto the fingerprint, making it pop right into view! "Amazing!" he said.

"In an actual investigation," Miss Hodges said, "you'd be taking close photographs of the fingerprints at each stage—before powdering, after powdering, before lifting, and after lifting."

"Lifting?" Ricky asked. "How do we do that? There's no way I can pick up this powder without messing it up."

"Yes, you can!" Miss Hodges said, smiling. "You're going to use a special tape."

With a little practice, the students found that they could lift the fingerprint right off the surface with a piece of tape. "Again, you've got to be very careful not to smear the print," Miss Hodges warned. "Keep your hands steady."

After they lifted the prints, the students stuck them onto cards and labeled them. If they'd used white powder, they taped the print to a black card. If they'd used black or gray powder, they used a white card.

"Does everyone have a card with at least one of your fingerprints on it?" Miss Hodges asked. They all did. "And are the cards labeled with your name, the date, and which finger you used?" A few students scribbled quickly and then nodded.

"Good," Miss Hodges said. "Now let's try using the fingerprints for identification." She split the class into groups of five. Each group had to choose one member to put a fingerprint on a glass slide. And it had to be a print from one of the same fingers the student had already recorded on a card.

As usual, Hannah, Ben, and Corey managed to be in a group together. Without saying it out loud, they chose Corey to put his thumbprint on a slide. They passed the slide around, so the other groups couldn't see who had made the print. (Actually, the other groups were too busy doing the same thing to notice.)

Miss Hodges then had each group pass their slide and their fingerprint cards to another group. That group had to examine the slide under a microscope and decide which card matched the fingerprint.

"If you pay really close attention to the lines in the fingerprint, it shouldn't be that hard to find the matches," Miss Hodges said as the class worked. "But remember, investigators aren't trying to match a fingerprint with just five other fingerprints. They're looking for a match in a database of *millions*. That's why they let computers do a lot of the work. But in the end it always comes down to a human expert to make the match."

As they walked out of the lab after the bell rang, Ben said to Hannah and Corey, "That was a great class."

"I know!" Hannah enthused. "It was like we were real crime-scene investigators."

"And you know where would probably be a great place to look for fingerprints?" Corey asked. "On a metal box!"

Chapter 6

C orey spent the whole weekend thinking about fingerprints. On Sunday evening he texted Ben and Hannah to ask them to meet him at his homeroom the next morning. So on Monday morning Ben and Hannah went to their homerooms early and got permission to visit Corey's homeroom. "Finally, we're in the same homeroom!" Corey said happily.

"Well, for one day," Ben said.

"It's a start," Corey said.

The three members of Club CSI had borrowed powders, brushes, tape, and cards from Miss Hodges. They explained to Mrs. Ramirez that they'd like to lift some fingerprints from the crime scene.

"Crime scene!" Mrs. Ramirez said. "I hadn't really thought of it that way."

"Has the thief returned the money?" Corey asked.

Mrs. Ramirez shook her head sadly. "I was hoping he or she would feel guilty and decide to do the right thing."

"You haven't called the police yet, have you?" Hannah asked.

"No," Mrs. Ramirez said. "I've told Principal Inverno, but we don't call the police for something relatively small like this, unless it's absolutely necessary."

"Well," Ben said, "we're not the police. But we're hoping we can help solve this theft."

Mrs. Ramirez thought a moment. "All right," she said. "Let's give it a try. I know everyone worked hard selling those magazine subscriptions, so it'd be a shame if they didn't get to contribute all the money they raised."

By now the other students had arrived in their homeroom. They were surprised to see Ben and Hannah up front, talking to their teacher.

"Class," Mrs. Ramirez said. "Corey and the two other members of—" She turned to Ben. "What was the name of your club again?"

"Club CSI," Ben answered.

Mrs. Ramirez turned back to the class. ". . . Club CSI are going to try to figure out who took the missing money. Let's watch as they show us some of the techniques Miss Hodges has taught them in her forensic science class."

As the whole class turned their attention to Club CSI, Ben, Hannah, and Corey felt a little uncomfortable. They hadn't known Mrs. Ramirez was going to turn this into a demonstration!

"I hope we remember how to do this right," Corey murmured.

"We will," Hannah said reassuringly. "Don't worry."

They started with the desk. It was light beige, so they chose the black powder. As they gently brushed the handle of the desk drawer that held the metal box, fingerprints clearly popped into view. Mrs. Ramirez was impressed.

"Very professional," she said. She invited the students to come up one by one to see the powdered fingerprints.

Throughout their investigation, Hannah took pictures with her phone.

After they'd found fingerprints with the powder, they lifted them with tape and attached them to

white cards. They wrote "Desk Drawer" on the cards to show where the prints had been found.

"Now, of course, you're going to find my fingerprints. I hope that's not going to lead to my arrest," said Mrs. Ramirez.

The students laughed.

Once Club CSI had gotten all the fingerprints they could off the drawer's handle, they asked Mrs. Ramirez to open the drawer and then take out the locked box. They used different powders to find fingerprints on the padlock and the box itself.

The metal surface of the box was an excellent place to find fingerprints. So was the back of the padlock. Many of the prints were smeared (lots of people had handled the box), but several were really clear.

As they worked on powdering the prints, the team got better at it. They felt good, as though they really were professional investigators.

The kids in the class watched, fascinated. "Just like on TV," one student murmured.

While the drawer was open, Hannah spotted something stuck in a crack between the drawer and the inside of the desk. She pulled it out.

"I think it's a feather," she said quietly. "Do you know where it came from?" she asked Mrs. Ramirez.

The homeroom teacher looked at the small feather. "No, I have no idea," she said.

Ben and Corey needed help with the fingerprints, so Hannah slipped the feather into a plastic bag and then stuck it in her pocket. She didn't want to make a big deal about the feather in front of the whole class. Everyone would probably have ideas about what it meant, and they didn't have time for a long discussion.

After they'd gotten all the fingerprints they could from the outside of the metal box and the padlock, they asked Mrs. Ramirez to open the box. Then they carefully took out Jacob's envelope, holding it by the edges.

"We really should have on gloves," Hannah said.

"You're right," Ben agreed. "Should have thought of that."

Paper wasn't nearly as good as metal for holding fingerprints, but they gave it a try. Hannah brushed on the black powder. A few fingerprints were faint, but they showed up.

They lifted them with tape and put them on

white cards, labeling them "Jacob Ritter's Envelope." Hannah included the date, too, wanting to be as professional as possible.

"Are those all the surfaces you wanted to cover?" Mrs. Ramirez asked. The club members looked at one another, then nodded.

"Now that you have all those fingerprints, what are you going to do with them?" she asked.

"Compare them," Corey said.

"Against what?" Mrs. Ramirez asked, puzzled.

"Well," Ben said, "we'd like to get fingerprints from everyone in your homeroom."

"We've brought ink pads and note cards," Hannah said, holding them out for Mrs. Ramirez to see.

"I see," Mrs. Ramirez said slowly. "I don't know."

"It won't take long," Ben said. "Making fingerprints with an ink pad is much quicker than lifting a print from a surface."

Corey turned to his classmates. "Is there anyone who doesn't want to be fingerprinted? Of course, I'm going to be fingerprinted too."

No one raised their hand. Corey, Ben, and Hannah had figured no one would refuse, even the thief. It would look suspicious. Of course, the thief might be nervous about being fingerprinted. They planned to watch everyone carefully to see if anyone was nervous.

But, actually, everyone seemed enthusiastic about the idea. They quickly lined up to be fingerprinted. As usual, Jean managed to be first.

As Club CSI had them roll their fingers across the ink pads and press them onto note cards, everyone seemed to be having fun. No one seemed nervous.

Ever competitive, Jacob tried to give the clearest, best fingerprint of all.

Even Mrs. Ramirez agreed to be fingerprinted.

Once they had everyone's fingerprints on note cards and had carefully labeled them, the members of Club CSI politely thanked the students and teacher for their cooperation.

The bell rang. "Well, that was certainly an interesting start to the day," Mrs. Ramirez said.

As the students walked out, Ben said, "What I'm really interested in are the comparisons. Do any of these cards hold the fingerprints of a thief?"

Chapter 7

Corey, Hannah, and Ben met in the forensics lab. Miss Hodges had given them permission to use the lab's magnifying glasses during a free period to compare the fingerprints they'd found at the crime scene with the fingerprints of Mrs. Ramirez and her students.

"So, what's the plan here, exactly?" Corey asked.

"We're going to see if any of the prints we lifted match the fingerprints on our cards, the ones with your classmates' names on them," Hannah said.

"Yeah, I get that," Corey said. "But how are we going to do it? We can't just start grabbing cards randomly."

Ben nodded. "Corey's right. We need some kind of system."

After talking about it, the three friends decided to divide the prints they'd lifted from the crime scene into three equal groups—one for each of them. "Each of us will try to identify all the fingerprints in our group," Ben said.

"We could call these the Mystery Prints," Corey said.

Next, they used the information Miss Hodges had taught them in class to put the labeled ink prints from the students and Mrs. Ramirez into groups. They spread the cards out on a table in the groups.

"And these are the Identified Prints. All we have to do is match up the Mystery Prints with the Identified Prints," Corey said.

"Right," Hannah agreed. "When you figure out who one of the Mystery Prints belongs to, write that person's name on the card."

Each of them took their stack of Mystery Prints and began looking at them carefully with a magnifying glass, comparing them, one by one, to the Identified Prints.

"Um, remind me," Corey said. "What's the difference between a whorl and a loop?"

"Target whorl or spiral whorl?" Ben asked.

"Either one," Corey said. "Surprise me."

"Well," Hannah said as she peered through her magnifying glass, "a loop is a ridge that just doubles back on itself. Kind of like the loop in your shoelaces."

"A whorl, on the other hand, is like a little whirlpool," Ben explained.

Corey said, "Right. I remember that. But you'd be amazed how few whirlpools I've seen growing up in Nevada."

"A target whorl looks like a target—a little circle with bigger circles around it," Hannah said.

"Got it," Corey said.

"And a spiral whorl looks kind of like a maze," Ben said. "One spiral winding around another spiral."

"Honestly? All these fingerprints kind of look like mazes," Corey said, looking through his magnifying glass.

Hannah looked up from her cards. "I don't know if this helps, but I start by looking at the center of the fingerprint to see if there's a little circle or two spirals. If there isn't, then I look for a loop. And if I don't see a nice curved loop, I look for an arch."

"Okay," Corey said. "That does help. I'll keep trying."

They stared through their magnifying glasses in

silence for a few minutes. Every once in a while one of them would walk over and trade one Identified Print for another. Then Corey cried out, "Aha!"

"Got a match?" Ben asked, excited.

"I think so," Corey said. "Pretty sure."

"Cool!" Hannah said.

Corey wrote the name of the matching student on the Mystery Print's card. The other two kept staring through their magnifying glasses. And staring. And staring . . .

"I wish we had a computer that could do this," Corey said, rubbing his eyes.

"Your homeroom classmates may be tough," Ben said, "but I doubt they're on file with the FBI."

Every once in a while, though, there'd be another "Ah!" or squeal of excitement from one of the investigators. And as they kept working, the cries started coming more often. "Match!" they'd say triumphantly.

They were getting much better at looking at fingerprints.

The more they stared at fingerprints, the more they got used to the different kinds of patterns the ridge lines could make. It was like staring at a lot of

maps until you could easily spot a park or a high-way interchange right away.

Slowly but surely, the three stacks of Mystery Prints were shrinking. The club members kept writing names on the cards and moving them into an "Identified" pile until there was just one Mystery Print left.

They'd found the same print on the desk drawer, on the metal box, on the padlock, and on Jacob's envelope.

And no matter how many times each of them tried comparing it to the Identified Prints, it never matched. It didn't seem to belong to any of the students or Mrs. Ramirez.

"You know what I think?" Hannah said, staring at the last Mystery Print.

"What?" Corey said.

"I think we're looking at the fingerprints of a thief," she said.

"So do I," Ben agreed.

"But these don't match anyone in the home-room," Corey said. "What good is having the thief's fingerprints if we don't know whose they are?"

That was a good question. It'd take forever to

get fingerprints from everyone in the school. They weren't even sure they could get permission to do that. And then it'd take even longer than it took that day to compare the Mystery Print to hundreds of other fingerprints.

"It's so frustrating," Hannah said. "We've got the thief's fingerprints, but we still don't have the thief."

"Still, we've made progress," Ben said.

"What do you mean?" Hannah asked.

"Now we're definitely sure the thief wasn't Mrs. Ramirez or any of her homeroom students," Ben said. "Someone who wasn't in that class opened the box. And why would someone else open the box unless they were meaning to steal the hundred dollars?"

"I'm innocent!" Corey added. "What a relief!"

"Were you really worried that you were guilty?" Hannah asked.

"Well," Corey said, "there's always sleepwalking. I might have stolen the money in my sleep."

"Do you sleepwalk?" Hannah asked.

"No, never," Corey said. "But there's always a first time."

The three of them stared at the Mystery Print for a while.

"Can we at least tell if these fingerprints belong to a kid or to an adult?" Corey asked.

"I don't think so," Ben said doubtfully. "I think that by the time you're our age, your fingers are pretty much full-size."

"Yeah, you're right," Corey agreed. "I can wear my dad's gloves, no problem."

"I hate to say it," Hannah said, "but we need more evidence."

"You're right," Ben said glumly.

They sat there, thinking. Then Corey piped up. "Hey," he said, "what about that feather?"

"What feather?" Ben asked.

"The one Hannah found in the desk drawer!" Corey said.

"You're right!" Hannah cried. "I'd forgotten all about it."

She rushed over to her backpack and then unzipped one of the smaller pockets. She reached in, pulling out a small plastic bag.

Inside was a single, small feather. It was mostly orange, with a little bit of brown. She took out the feather and held it up. The three friends studied it.

"Is it a bird's feather?" Corey asked.

Ben turned to look at his friend. "What other kind is there?"

"Well," Corey said, thinking, "there are the feathers that come from feather dusters."

"Those are bird's feathers," Ben said.

"Or the feathers they put in pillows," Corey said.

"Again, bird," Ben said.

"Aren't some old-fashioned pens made from feathers?" Corey asked.

"Yes," Ben said. "Bird's feathers."

Hannah was still examining the feather. "Staring at this little feather tells me basically . . . nothing," she said. "But I know someone who might have some suggestions."

Chapter 8

Miss Hodges held up the little feather to the light in her office and turned it this way and that, examining it. "Well," she said after a moment, "I'm not a feather expert. But I do know a *few* things about them."

"Such as?" Hannah asked eagerly.

"To start with, birds have several different kinds of feathers," she explained. "Two of the main types are tail feathers and wing feathers."

"Makes sense," Ben said.

"Within wing feathers, there are primary feathers and secondary feathers," Miss Hodges went on. "The primary feathers are closer to the tip of the wing, and the secondary feathers are closer to the bird's body."

"Okay, you're kind of starting to sound like a feather expert," Corey said, looking suspicious.

Miss Hodges laughed. "Not at all! The world of feathers is big and complicated. There are, for example, all the different parts of the feather."

"A feather looks like just one part to me," Corey said. "If you put it together with the other parts—beak, claws, more feathers—you get a bird."

"Look closely," Miss Hodges said. She used her finger to separate the individual strands of the feather. "These strands are called barbs."

She ran her finger along the center of the feather, toward the tip. "The barbs are attached to the shaft. The upper part of the shaft, toward the tip, is called the rachis."

She pointed to the bottom of the feather. "And the other end of the shaft is called the calamus, or the quill."

"Like a quill pen," Ben said.

"Exactly!" Miss Hodges said. "Each side of the feather is called a vane."

"Like a weather vane?" Hannah asked.

Miss Hodges nodded.

"Only this is a feather vane," Corey said, smiling.

"Right," Miss Hodges said. "All these features, and, of course, the colors, help a real feather expert identify what kind of a bird the feather came from."

She handed the feather back to Hannah, who looked at it with new understanding. Miss Hodges turned to her computer.

"Let me show you a really neat website," she said. "It's from the US Fish and Wildlife Service. They have their own forensics lab to help solve crimes involving wildlife."

"Like when a gang of raccoons knocks over a garbage can?" Corey asked.

"No, Corey," Miss Hodges said patiently. "In these cases, the animals are the victims. The criminals are usually poachers and people trying to sell protected species."

She clicked her mouse a couple of times. "Here we are," she said. "This is the feather atlas. You can use it to identify feathers."

"Perfect!" Hannah said.

Miss Hodges got up from her chair and motioned for Hannah to take her place. "It's easy to use. Just click on 'Identify Feather' and go from there. I'll be in the lab if you need me."

Club CSI got down to work. They started by picking one of eight patterns that best matched their feather. Then they clicked on "orange," since that was the feather's main color. This gave them ten results, including woodpeckers, flickers, and thrushes.

But none of them really matched.

They tried some other combinations of pattern and color, but they just couldn't find any feathers that looked exactly like their mystery feather.

"Frustrating," Corey grumbled.

"The website says it doesn't cover every kind of bird there is," Ben pointed out. "They're still adding more birds all the time."

"Let's tell Miss Hodges," Hannah said. "Maybe she'll have an idea."

They went into the lab and found Miss Hodges grading papers. "No luck," Ben said. "None of the birds matched our feather."

"Hmm," Miss Hodges said. "Well, since the website comes from the US Fish and Wildlife Service, it covers only wild birds. Maybe the feather isn't from a wild bird."

"You mean it's from a pet bird?" Corey asked. "Like a parakeet?"

"Maybe," Miss Hodges said. "Or some other kind of domesticated bird."

"Like what?" Hannah asked.

"Well, think," Miss Hodges said, always the teacher. "What kind of birds have we humans domesticated?"

Ben thought. "Chickens," he said. "Turkeys. Maybe ducks."

"Good!" Miss Hodges said. "Let me see that feather again, please."

Hannah handed her the feather. As Miss Hodges studied it, she said, "As I look at the colors of this feather again, I'm wondering if maybe this might be a rooster feather."

"Why would anyone have a rooster feather in Mrs. Ramirez's classroom?" Corey wondered out loud.

"I've got an idea," Hannah said. "Let's do a quick Internet search on rooster feathers to see what comes up."

"Good idea," Miss Hodges said, nodding.

They hurried back into Miss Hodges's office. Almost immediately, they found that rooster feathers are used to make flies for fly-fishing.

"Fly-fishing?" Corey said. "You know, Mike Crowley

talks about fly-fishing all the time. Remember?"

"Yeah," Ben said. "We were talking about him at lunch in the cafeteria."

"All right! Let's find Mike Crowley!" Hannah said, starting off without them. Ben and Corey hurried after her.

They spotted Mike by his locker. "Hey, Mike!" Corey called.

Mike turned to the three members of Club CSI running toward him. "Yeah?" he asked, having no idea what was going on.

"We just wondered if we could talk to you for a second about fly-fishing," Ben asked.

Mike looked at the three of them, trying to figure out if they were kidding. He'd been talking so much about his new favorite activity that kids had started to tease him a little. "Really?" he said suspiciously.

"Yeah, really," Hannah said. "We just were wondering about how you make your own flies."

"Well," Mike said. "It's pretty hard. You need special equipment and tools, and you have to know how to tie these special knots. You need steady hands."

"What kind of materials do you use?" Corey asked innocently. If Mike was the thief, Corey didn't want to tip him off that they were on to him.

Mike set his backpack on the floor next to his locker. "There's the hook. And different kinds of thread. And the hackles."

Hannah looked puzzled. "What are hackles?"

"They're feathers—little feathers that you tie onto the hook," Mike explained. "I think they're supposed to look like wings."

The members of Club CSI exchanged a look. "Wow, I've never seen one of those," Hannah said. "Could you show me one?"

"Sure," Mike said. "I'd have to borrow one from my uncle, though. He's the one who ties his own flies."

Ben frowned. "You mean you've never tied one yourself?"

"No, it's really hard," Mike admitted. "He's going to teach me."

"Did you ever bring any of those feathers to school?" Corey asked.

"Nope, I never did," Mike answered, surprised. "Why would I?" He looked and sounded as though he were telling the truth.

"No reason," Corey said, disappointed. "Well, thanks."

"Sure," Mike said, confused. "I'll ask my uncle if I can borrow one of his flies to bring in and show you. You can see what hackles are for yourselves."

"That's okay," Hannah said. "I just thought maybe if you had one with you, I could look at it, but you don't have to go to any trouble."

"It's no trouble," Mike said with a friendly grin.

"Well, that was pretty much a complete waste of time," Corey said quietly as they walked away.

"It really seemed as though he were telling the truth," Ben said. "He never brought any rooster feathers to school."

"And now I'm going to have to act interested when he brings a fishing lure to school to show me," Hannah complained. "And I *hate* fishing. So gross."

They walked on in silence, thinking. How did that feather get in Mrs. Ramirez's desk? Had the thief dropped it?

"I keep thinking I've seen feathers somewhere recently," Hannah said. Then she stopped right in her tracks. "Wait! I know where I saw feathers!"

"Where?" Corey asked. "On a pirate?"

Ben turned to Corey, baffled. "Pirate?"

"Yeah," Corey said. "From the parrot on his shoulder."

"You have an amazing brain," Ben said.

"Thank you," Corey said.

"I remember where I've been seeing feathers lately," Hannah said, excited.

"Where?" Ben asked.

"In girls' hair!"

Chapter 9

"W ait," Ben said to Hannah. "You're saying you saw rooster feathers in some girl's hair?"

"Like a nest?" Corey asked, completely baffled.

"Not in just one girl's hair," Hannah said. "In several girls' hair. It's a trend in hairstyling—feather extensions. I just read a magazine article about it last week at the doctor's office."

Hannah explained to the two boys, who were completely clueless about fashion, that some girls were tying feathers to their hair. Since reading that article, she'd noticed more than one girl at Woodlands Junior High with feathers in her hair. The feathers weren't really obvious most of the time, because girls often got ones that matched their hair color. But some girls chose to get wild colors that stood out in bright streaks against their hair.

"I see," Corey said. "Well, based on what Mike told us, they'd better be careful when they walk by streams and rivers. Trout might come jumping out to bite their hair."

As they walked through the hallways, the three friends kept their eyes peeled for girls with feathers woven into their hair. It wasn't long before they spotted a couple.

"Okay, I get it," Ben said. "But just because these girls have feathers in their hair today doesn't mean they had them back when our feather dropped into Mrs. Ramirez's desk."

"True," Hannah said.

"How long can you leave the feathers in your hair?" Corey asked. "I mean, don't you have to wash your hair?"

"The article said you can wash the feathers," Hannah said. "Which makes sense. Birds do it all the time."

"I guess you're right," Corey conceded.

"And the feathers can last more than a month," she added.

Corey remembered one of the girls with feathers in her hair from his homeroom. "Her name is . . . um . . . let me think," he said. "Starts with an *A* . . . Ava!"

"That's funny," Ben said.

"What's funny about the name Ava?" Hannah asked.

"I think it comes from 'avis,'" he said.

"The car rental company?" Corey said.

"No, the Latin word for 'bird,'" Ben said. "Maybe that's why she likes having feathers in her hair."

"Or maybe she thinks it looks cool," Hannah said, shrugging. "Come on. Let's find out how long she's had them."

The three of them strolled casually over to Ava. "Hi, Ava," Corey said. "How's it going?"

Ava smiled. She knew Corey from homeroom. And she'd always thought he was cute.

"Good!" she said. "What's up?"

"I love the feathers in your hair," Hannah said.

"Oh, thanks!" Ava chirped. "I wasn't sure which color to get at first, but then I really liked these."

Hannah took one of the feathers in her hand. "This color's great. It's kind of like orange and brown."

She gave Ben and Corey a quick look. Ava's

feathers were the same colors as the feather they'd found in Mrs. Ramirez's desk.

"Can you wash your hair with those in it?" Corey asked.

Ava blushed. "Of course. Birds wash their feathers, you know."

Ben smiled at Ava. "Could you excuse us for just a second, Ava?"

She looked puzzled. "Um, sure."

Ben took Hannah and Corey by their arms and stepped a few steps away from Ava. "She's not the thief," he said in a low voice.

"But her feathers match the one in the desk," Hannah argued.

"I know," Ben said. "But I just remembered that we have her fingerprints. I checked them myself. They don't match the Mystery Print. And those are the fingerprints we're pretty sure belong to the thief, remember?"

Hannah nodded. "Yeah, you're right. But we should still try to figure out whether the feather came from Ava."

"Agreed," Corey said, wanting to contribute something to this discussion.

They walked back to Ava.

"Sorry about that," Ben said.

"That's okay," Ava said, still a little confused.

"Look," Hannah said. "We'll be honest with you. We're investigating the missing hundred dollars."

Ava looked nervous. "Well, I didn't take it!" she insisted.

"We know," Corey said. "But we found a feather in Mrs. Ramirez's desk. Could it have come from your hair?"

"I don't know," Ava said. "Can I see it?"

"Sure," Hannah said. She dug around in her backpack and came up with the plastic bag holding the feather. She opened the bag, took out the feather, and handed it to Ava.

Ava looked at the feather. Then she held it next to one of the feathers in her hair, comparing the colors. They were the same.

"It does look the same," she admitted, handing it back to Hannah. "I guess it could have come from my hair."

"Have you been by Mrs. Ramirez's desk recently?" Ben asked.

Ava thought a minute. Then her face brightened.

"Yeah," she said. "I went up by her desk to turn in my magazine subscription money, just like everybody else. Maybe it fell off then."

The three friends nodded. That made perfect sense.

Unfortunately, it didn't get them any closer to catching the thief.

"Thanks, Ava," Corey said. "You've been a big help."

"I have?" she asked. "Great." She stood there grinning at Corey, who smiled back awkwardly.

"Well," he said, "we should probably get going. See you in homeroom."

"See you."

The members of Club CSI turned and started to walk away. But then Ava called to them.

"Oh, hey!" she said. "Can I have my feather back?"

Hannah looked at Ben and Corey. They nodded. The feather wasn't really of any use to them now that they were pretty sure it didn't come from the thief.

"Sure," Hannah said, handing Ava the feather.

"Thanks," Ava said. "And good luck with your investigation."

"Thanks," Ben said. "I think we're going to need it."

Chapter 10

The three members of Club CSI sat in a school hallway that didn't get much traffic. It led past some dusty cases full of old trophies to an exit that was kept locked.

They looked discouraged. Mainly because they *were* discouraged.

They had found a set of fingerprints they believed belonged to the thief. But they didn't know whose fingerprints they were.

They had found a feather at the crime scene, but instead of an important clue, it had turned out to be a dead end. Like this hallway.

Corey tossed a ball up and caught it, over and over. Hannah twisted a strap on her backpack.

Ben decided they needed some cheering up.

"Remember what Miss Hodges says," he said.

"Leave investigating crime to the professionals?" Corey asked.

"I don't think I remember her ever saying that," Hannah said.

"Well, maybe she should have," Corey countered.

"No," Ben said. "She says to keep asking questions. As long as you've got another question to answer, your investigation is still alive."

That was true. Hannah and Corey thought about what Ben had said. And then something occurred to Hannah.

"I've got a question," she said.

"Okay," Ben said. "Let's hear it."

"How did the thief steal the hundred dollars when the metal box it was in was locked?" she asked.

"Yeah," Corey said, stopping his throwing for a minute. "And the desk drawer was locked too."

"That's a good question," Ben said. "The locks didn't look broken, so I'm guessing the thief picked them somehow."

"So maybe we should be looking for someone who knows about locks," Hannah suggested.

"Is it hard to pick locks?" Corey asked. "You hear

people talking about picking locks, but I really have no idea how to do it."

"Neither do I," Hannah said. "Do you need some kind of special tools? Maybe the tools would lead us to the thief."

Ben stood up. "I think we need to know more about locks and how to pick them. Maybe Miss Hodges will have an idea."

Corey stood up too. "Well, if she knows as much about locks as she does about feathers, we should be all set."

Hannah stood up, and they headed down the hall toward Miss Hodges's office.

Miss Hodges was busy preparing her classes for the next week. But when the Club CSI members told her what they were interested in, she had an answer for them right away.

"You should go see my friend Chuck," she said.

"Who's he?" Corey asked.

"A locksmith," Miss Hodges answered. She wrote something on a piece of paper and then handed it to Corey. "Here's his address. It's not far."

Hannah half expected the locksmith shop to be a dark, greasy, dirty place. But when they opened the front door, they saw a clean, brightly lit store where everything seemed to be in place.

The older man behind the counter looked up from the lock he was working on, and smiled. "Afternoon!" he said. "May I help you?"

"We'd like to know how to pick locks!" Corey blurted out.

The smile disappeared from the man's face. "Well, I'm afraid I'm not going to be able to help you with that, kids."

Ben tried to explain. "We're students in Miss Hodges's forensic science class. She said you might be able to help us understand locks better, so we could figure out who stole some money at school."

"Are you Chuck?" Hannah asked, trying her best to look nothing like a robber who planned to pick people's locks.

"I sure am," Chuck said, smiling again. "And Miss Hodges is a good friend of mine. If she said I should help you, then I guess it's all right."

"We appreciate it," Ben said. "We realize we know pretty much nothing about locks."

"Then we'll start with the basics," Chuck said. He reached down behind the counter and picked up a board with several labeled locks on it. He pointed to the different kinds of locks as he named them.

"Pin-and-tumbler lock, wafer tumbler lock, tubular lock, padlock . . ." The world of locks, like the world of feathers, seemed to be a big one. Chuck explained how some of the locks were much more difficult to pick than others.

"So," he said. "This thief of yours. What kind of lock did he or she pick?"

"Well, first he or she picked the lock on a desk drawer," Hannah said.

"Like a teacher's desk? At school?" Chuck asked.

"Yes," Corey said.

"Wooden or metal?" Chuck asked.

"Wood," Corey said. "I mean, the desk was wood. The lock was metal. Of course."

"Old or new?"

Corey thought a minute. "Old, I think. It looks kind of scratched and beat up."

"Kind of like me!" Chuck said, laughing. "I'd have

to see the lock to know exactly what kind it is. But I'm guessing it wouldn't be too hard to pick."

"Oh!" Hannah said suddenly. "I just remembered something! I have pictures of the lock on my phone."

She dug out her phone from her backpack and then started searching through her recent photos until she found a decent close-up of the lock on Mrs. Ramirez's desk drawer. She handed her phone to Chuck.

Lowering his reading glasses, he peered at the image on the small screen. "Okay, yeah," he said. "That's pretty much what I'd imagined. Not much of a lock, I'm afraid. It wouldn't take an expert to pick that open with a small screwdriver and a paper clip." He used his fingers to make the picture bigger. "In fact, I think I can make out scratch marks on the face of the lock. That'd be consistent with a screwdriver."

In his mind Ben scolded himself for not examining the lock more closely. He should have looked at it with a magnifying glass. But to tell the truth, he'd been a little shy about using one in front of Corey's homeroom classmates. He was afraid they'd think he was trying to be Sherlock Holmes. Even though he actually was.

"So, just to be clear, you're saying it wouldn't take any special tools or skills to pick open the lock on the desk drawer," Hannah said.

"Exactly," Chuck said, nodding.

"That's too bad," Corey said. "It doesn't really help us track down the thief. Pretty much anyone could get their hands on a screwdriver and a paper clip."

"That's true," Chuck said. "Anything else I can help you with?"

Hannah found another picture on her phone and showed it to Chuck. "There was another lock, a padlock."

Chuck glanced at the picture. "Right. I know that brand. I carry it myself." He leaned down, reaching into the display counter and pulling out a padlock just like the one on Mrs. Ramirez's metal box.

"Now this lock," he said, holding up the lock, "would be very hard to pick."

"Then how did the thief get the box open?" Corey asked.

"Could he or she have known the combination?" Chuck asked.

"Good question," Ben said.

As they walked away from Chuck's locksmith shop, the three friends talked about what they'd learned.

"Who might know the combination to the padlock?" Hannah asked. "Did Mrs. Ramirez tell it to anyone?"

"Or did she maybe write it down and leave it somewhere, and the thief found it?" Ben asked.

Corey thought about this, then shook his head. "I don't think so," he said. "I doubt Mrs. Ramirez would tell anyone the combination. And since she has a great memory for numbers, she wouldn't need to write it down. Besides, she used a formula to come up with the combination."

Ben stopped walking along the sidewalk and turned toward Corey, excited. "What formula?"

"I don't remember," Corey said. "I just remember her telling us the formula. It was kind of like an equation or a math puzzle."

"Did you figure it out?" Hannah asked.

"I didn't even try," Corey said. "I don't like math puzzles. I can barely get all my math homework done as it is. I don't want to do extra math just for fun."

Ben started off down the sidewalk at a brisk pace.

"Where are you going?" Hannah called after him.

"Back to Mrs. Ramirez," he yelled back over his shoulder. "It's not quite five yet. Maybe she's still in her classroom."

Hannah and Corey hurried after him.

Chapter 11

N o," Mrs. Ramirez said, shaking her head emphatically. "I definitely did not write down the combination. Anywhere."

Corey nodded. "That's what I told them."

"We just have to cover all the bases," Ben said apologetically. "It's good to know the thief couldn't have found the combination written down."

Hannah, Corey, and Ben were in Mrs. Ramirez's classroom. She had been grading quizzes when they found her. But she was happy to pause a little while to answer their questions. She wanted the missing money returned just as much as her students did. And grading quizzes wasn't her favorite activity.

"And so you had the combination memorized," Hannah said.

"Yes," Mrs. Ramirez answered. "And it was easy to remember."

"Did you tell anyone the combination?" Ben asked.

"No," Mrs. Ramirez said. "But I did tell my students the formula for the combination."

"Yes, Corey mentioned that," Ben said. "What was the formula?"

Mrs. Ramirez got up and walked over to the dry-erase board. "Well," she began, "every year with my homeroom class, I use this formula as a learning exercise."

She picked up a marker and then wrote "First number = even."

"The first number in the padlock combination is an even number," she said.

"Okay," Ben said, writing in a small notebook he carried with him at all times so he could keep track of clues.

Mrs. Ramirez wrote "Second number = (First number/two) squared" on the board.

"The second number is the first number divided by two and then squared—multiplied by itself," she explained.

"Got it," Ben said, writing.

Finally, the teacher wrote "Third number = First number + Second number."

"The third number is the sum of the first two numbers," she finished.

"Oh yeah," Corey said. "I remember this now. I didn't know the answer the first time, and I don't know the answer now."

Corey sometimes thought his brain just wasn't made the right way to get math. But then he'd look at some NBA player's stats, and he'd understand them perfectly. So maybe it wasn't just his brain. Maybe it had something to do with what he was interested in.

"There are several possible correct answers," Ben said.

"Yes," Mrs. Ramirez said. "That's right."

Hannah carefully looked at what Mrs. Ramirez had written on the board. "It seems to me that the formula would be easy to figure out if you knew one of the numbers," Hannah noted.

Mrs. Ramirez agreed. "If you were just trying to guess the answer, you'd have to go through quite a few combinations. But if you knew one of the three numbers, you could easily figure out the other two."

Ben thought for a moment. Then he asked, "What's the last number?"

Mrs. Ramirez hesitated. "I've always kept that information a secret. But I suppose it doesn't matter now."

"Now that the thief knows your combination, I guess you'll have to change it, anyway," Corey pointed out.

She nodded. "Yes, that's right. So I might as well tell you three. The last number is 35."

"So the combination was 10, 25, 35," Ben said quickly.

Corey's mouth dropped open. "How did you figure that out so quickly? Did you secretly use a calculator?"

"No," Ben said. "It's just algebra. Think of the numbers as X, Y, and Z. Then plug in 35 for Z, and solve for X and Y."

"I think I'd rather just think of your brain as freakishly big," Corey said.

Hannah asked Mrs. Ramirez if Ben was right. She nodded. "Absolutely. That's the correct answer, and the combination that opens the padlock."

"So Ben was able to figure out the combination once he knew the last number," Hannah said. "But

how would the thief have known any of the numbers?"

"Do you say the numbers to yourself as you turn the dial on the padlock?" Corey asked. "Because maybe the thief could read lips."

Mrs. Ramirez smiled. "Well, I'm not completely sure, but I don't think I move my lips as I turn the dial."

Ben got an idea. "Did you spin the dial after you locked the padlock?"

"You mean when I put the box away on Monday morning?" Mrs. Ramirez asked. Ben nodded. She frowned, trying to remember.

"That's quite a few days ago now," she said, thinking. "I can't really be sure whether I spun the dial or not. Do you remember, Corey?"

Corey thought back to last Monday morning. He vaguely remembered Mrs. Ramirez putting the metal box in her desk drawer after everyone had put their envelopes of money in it, but he didn't remember whether or not she spun the dial on the padlock.

"I really don't remember," Corey said. "She could have spun the dial on the padlock after it was below the top of her desk, so we couldn't see."

"I don't think I would do that," Mrs. Ramirez said. "Once I picked up the metal box, I would probably hold it in one hand while I opened my desk drawer with my other hand. I wouldn't have a hand free to spin the dial on the combination lock."

Ben and Hannah listened to all this and thought about it. "My guess is," Ben said slowly, "that you didn't spin the dial on the combination lock after you closed it."

"So the dial was still set on the combination's final number, 35," Hannah added.

"Right," agreed Ben. "All the thief had to do was look at the dial to see the final number. Then he or she would just have to use the formula to figure out the first two numbers in the combination."

"Okay," Corey said. "But that means the thief had to know the formula. And Mrs. Ramirez only tells the formula to the kids in her homeroom. Right?"

Mrs. Ramirez nodded.

"Except the fingerprints already showed us that the thief is probably someone from outside our homeroom," Corey reminded them.

Ben and Hannah looked stumped for a minute. Then Hannah remembered something. "Mrs. Ramirez, didn't you say that you use this formula with your homeroom every year?"

"Yes," she agreed. "I've been using it for several years now."

"I see where you're going with this, Hannah," Ben said. "Maybe the thief was in Mrs. Ramirez's homeroom in a previous year."

"Right!" Hannah said. "Like last year, so you might still remember the formula. The thief might be an eighth grader."

"Maybe we should fingerprint all the eighth graders!" Corey said.

Ben held up his hands. "We really just need the kids from Mrs. Ramirez's homeroom last year, but I think we should run this theory by Miss Hodges before we try to get permission to fingerprint any more students."

"That sounds like an excellent idea, Ben," Mrs. Ramirez said.

"Well, what are we waiting for?" Hannah said. "Let's go!"

She hurried out of the classroom. Ben and Corey followed her. At the door, Corey turned back to Mrs. Ramirez. "Thanks, Mrs. Ramirez!" he said.

"You're welcome!" she said, turning back to grading the stack of quizzes with a little sigh.

Hannah, Ben, and Corey got to school extra early the next morning, eager to bounce their latest theory off Miss Hodges before homeroom.

She wasn't impressed.

"It's a pretty good theory," she said. "But it's not conclusive. I'm afraid it's never going to convince Principal Inverno to let you get fingerprints from all the eighth graders."

Hannah and Ben looked disappointed. Secretly, Corey was relieved. He hadn't been looking forward to pressing all those eighth graders' fingers onto ink pads and then onto cards. Not to mention having to compare all those fingerprints to the unidentified set of prints they'd taken off the metal box and the desk drawer handle. He felt like his eyes were still tired from the first round of fingerprint comparisons.

"Well," Ben said, "in that case, it seems as though we've hit another dead end. The padlock combination didn't lead us to the thief."

"No, it didn't," Miss Hodges said. "But that's not usually how evidence works. You're not just looking for the one thing that'll lead you directly to the criminal. You're building up a case, fact by fact. The more you know, the closer you are to solving the crime."

That made them feel a little better. But what should they do next? It seemed as though they had run out of trails to follow. They asked Miss Hodges for advice.

"Well," she replied, "I believe I would think about motive next."

"Motive?" Corey asked.

"Yes," she said. "Money has been stolen. Why? What did the thief want that hundred dollars for?"

Club CSI thanked Miss Hodges for her advice.

During their free period, Ben, Hannah, and Corey met to discuss the case. It turned out that all three of them couldn't stop thinking about why the thief had stolen the hundred dollars.

"I'm thinking the thief wanted to spend the money on something specific," Ben said.

"Why?" Hannah asked.

"Because he or she took a specific amount," he answered. "There was more than a thousand dollars in that metal box. But instead of just grabbing it all, the thief took only one hundred dollars."

They thought about this as they walked down the hallway. "So we're looking for someone who wanted to buy something specific and only needed one hundred dollars to buy it," Corey said.

"I think so," Ben said.

"It makes sense," Hannah said. "But that person is going to be tough to find. Kids in this school buy stuff that cost at least a hundred dollars all the time."

"I think it's worth a try," Corey said. "We should be on the lookout for someone who has something new. Something they've gotten recently. And that costs more than a hundred dollars."

"Yeah," Ben agreed. "Unless they bought something that cost less than a hundred dollars and then kept the change."

"It could be," Hannah said. "But like you said, they could easily have taken more than a hundred dollars. So the thief probably stole just the amount of money he or she needed."

They'd reached Corey's homeroom. "Okay," he said. "We'll meet up again at lunch. In the meantime I'll keep my eyes peeled for kids with new, expensive stuff."

"So will I," Ben said.

"Me too," Hannah chimed in. "See you at lunch."

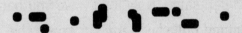

Between the next two periods, Ben noticed a kid from his English class wearing a backpack with headphones plugged into one of the arm straps.

"Excuse me," Ben said to him. "Can you plug your headphones right into your backpack?"

"What?" the kid asked. He couldn't hear Ben with his earbuds stuck in his ears. He had his music turned up so loud that Ben could hear it.

Ben motioned for the kid to take out at least

one of his earbuds. After the kid had removed the left earbud, Ben repeated his question.

The kid grinned. "Yeah," he said proudly. "I can put my MP3 player in this pocket. Then I plug the earbuds in here." He showed Ben the place on the strap where the plug went in. "I can even adjust the volume—see?"

The backpack had a volume control on the strap too.

"I'm thinking about getting one of these," Ben said casually. "How much do they cost?"

The kid shrugged. "I don't know. My uncle gave it to me."

"Oh," Ben said. "How long have you had it?"

"Since my birthday. Like, three months. Why?"

"I just wondered if it was durable," Ben said, improvising. The kid seemed to buy it.

"Very durable," the kid said, nodding. "And cool." He stuck the bud back into his ear and walked away.

Three months. Long before the thief had taken the money.

Corey spotted the shoes from across the room. New basketball shoes. Really nice ones. When class was over, he went up to the kid wearing them, a guy named Tyler.

"Nice kicks," he said.

"Nice what?" Tyler asked.

"Kicks," Corey repeated. It was something he'd heard his dad say as a joke. "Shoes."

"Huh," Tyler said. "Kicks. I've never heard that." He started to walk away.

"I was thinking about getting a pair of those," Corey said. "How much are they?"

Tyler stopped and thought.

"Um, like a hundred and twenty-five dollars," he said.

"Wow, that's a lot," Corey said.

Tyler shrugged. "Shoes are expensive. This style might cost even more now. I got them, like, almost a year ago."

"But they look new," Corey said.

Tyler shrugged again. "I take good care of my kicks."

Hannah wasn't really into purses, but she knew a nice one when she saw it. This one had fringe hanging from the front of it, which made it dance back and forth on the arm of a skinny girl with blond hair who was walking quickly down the hallway.

Hannah quickened her pace, falling in step beside the girl. She turned and glared at Hannah. "May I help you?" she asked.

"Sorry," Hannah said. "I was just admiring your purse. Is it real leather?"

The girl smiled. "Thanks! Yeah. I just got it."

That was promising. "Would you mind if I asked you how much it cost?" Hannah asked.

"Well," the girl said, looking a little embarrassed. "It was actually on this huge sale. And my mom had a coupon. So it was only about thirty dollars."

Even though she was disappointed by the girl's answer, Hannah managed to look very enthusiastic. "Wow! What a great deal! You must be a brilliant shopper!"

The girl looked a little puzzled. "Thank you," she said. "I guess."

At lunch, Corey was talking to Ben between bites of turkey.

"You know," Corey said with food in his mouth, "I never really noticed before, but the kids in this school have a lot of new stuff. If you start looking for it, you see it everywhere."

"Tell me about it," Ben agreed. "I'm starting to think the students at Woodlands Junior High are a little too into buying things."

Corey took a long drink of milk. "Do you think any of the stuff you saw was bought with stolen money?"

Ben shook his head. "Not really. I mean, I guess it could have been, but everything I asked about was either bought long before the theft or given to the person as a gift."

Corey nodded. "Yeah, me too. And I'm starting to feel kind of uncomfortable asking people where they got things. They must think I'm really weird."

"They already think I'm weird," Ben said.

"No, they don't," Corey said, coming to the defense of his friend, even though he knew that some kids in the school *did* think Ben was weird. To change the subject, he asked, "Where's Hannah?"

"I don't know," Ben said. Then he spotted her approaching their table. "Here she comes."

"And she looks excited!" Corey noticed.

Chapter 13

Hannah plopped down into a seat next to Corey and Ben. She just smiled at them for a moment, enjoying knowing something they didn't know yet.

"Well?" Corey asked.

"What'd you find out?" Ben asked, leaning forward.

"At first I tried just keeping my eyes peeled for new stuff, but that didn't really work," she said. "The kids in this school buy a ton of new stuff."

"We were actually just talking about that," Corey said, nodding.

"So instead of just walking through the halls and classrooms trying to spot someone with something expensive, I started asking around," she continued.

Ben suspected it was easier for a girl to "ask

around" than it was for a guy, but he didn't say anything.

"Can I have one of your chips?" Hannah asked Corey.

"Yeah," he said. "One."

She took a chip and crunched it. "So I found out that there's this eighth grader named Brittney who just got one of those Quark Pads."

Ben looked doubtful. "A lot of kids have those."

"Yeah, pretty much everyone except me," Corey complained.

"But listen to how she got it," Hannah said, sneaking one of Corey's chips. "It was given to her as a gift by this eighth-grade boy who likes her named Greg Marshall."

Corey whistled. "Wow, that's a nice gift. He must *really* like her."

"Yeah, it's such a nice gift that Brittney's mom wouldn't let her keep it," Hannah said.

"Wait," Corey said. "So she had to give it back? I'll take it!"

"When Brittney tried to give the Quark Pad back to Greg, he said, 'You have no idea what I went through to get that for you!'" Hannah went on, relishing this part of the story.

"He said that? An eighth grader?" Ben asked, hanging on every word.

"Yep," she said. "And then he ran off without taking back the Quark Pad."

All three of them thought about this story. It was very interesting. "I think maybe we should talk to Brittney," Ben said.

"That shouldn't be too hard," Hannah said. "She's eating lunch right over there."

Hannah pointed at a pretty, red-haired girl sitting a few tables away. Ben got up right away and started walking over to her. Corey and Hannah followed close behind him.

When he reached the table, Brittney looked up curiously. "Yes?"

Now that he was face-to-face with this eighth-grade girl, Ben wasn't sure what to say. He turned to Hannah and let her take over.

"Hi," Hannah said. "My name's Hannah. You're Brittney, right?"

The girl nodded. Hannah asked her if the story about Greg Marshall and the Quark Pad was true.

Brittney looked embarrassed. "I can't believe everyone's talking about this. I do not want to be

Greg Marshall's girlfriend. He's just a big, weird guy."

"Do you still have the Quark Pad?" Corey asked.

"Yeah," Brittney said. "He wouldn't take it back. But my mom doesn't want me to keep it. I'm not sure what to do with it."

"May we borrow it for a little while?" Ben asked.

Brittney looked confused. "What for?"

Hannah explained that they were Club CSI and that they thought the Quark Pad might be an important clue in an investigation. Shrugging, Brittney handed the Quark Pad to Hannah. Ben stopped Hannah before she took it.

"Careful," he said. "Try to handle it by the edges."

"I'll do better than that," Hannah said. She took rubber gloves out of her backpack, put them on, and took the Quark Pad.

"To the laboratory!" Corey said. "I've always wanted to say that."

The three friends quickly borrowed the materials they needed from Miss Hodges. Then they started working on getting fingerprints from the Quark Pad.

"There are fingerprints all over it!" Corey said.

"Yeah," Ben said as he carefully applied powder. "The glass surface is perfect for fingerprints."

"A lot of these fingerprints are probably going to be Brittney's," Hannah observed.

"True, but I'm hoping Greg Marshall's are still on here too," Ben said.

It didn't take them long to find a set of fingerprints that matched the Mystery Print they found on the box the money was stolen from.

"That's it!" Corey said. "If these are Greg's fingerprints, then he must be the thief!"

"Well, it's not definite," Ben said cautiously. "There could be another explanation. But it does seem pretty likely."

"What do we do next?" Hannah asked. "We can't just walk up to Greg Marshall and say, 'Um, excuse me, but did you happen to steal a hundred dollars from the locked box in Mrs. Ramirez's homeroom?'"

"Didn't Brittney say Greg is big?" Corey asked.

"And weird," Ben added.

"And an eighth grader," Hannah said.

They sat there for a minute, thinking. It didn't sound like it would be much fun to accuse some big, weird, older guy of stealing money.

"Maybe we should just pass this information along to Miss Hodges or Principal Inverno and let them handle it," Ben suggested.

"But then Club CSI wouldn't get credit for catching the thief," Corey protested.

"Besides," Hannah said, "I don't think this counts as proof that Greg stole the money. I think we need more information."

"From where?" Corey asked.

"From Greg," Hannah said.

They were quiet again, trying to decide what to do now.

"So we're right back to confronting a big, weird eighth grader," Corey said gloomily.

"At least there'll be three of us," Ben pointed out. "And we could try to talk to him someplace where there are a lot of other people around."

"You know, we don't even know what this guy looks like," Corey said. "I'm picturing something kind of like a cross between Frankenstein and Napoleon Dynamite."

"Okay," Hannah said. "Let's do it tomorrow. First thing in the morning, I'll try to find Brittney and ask her to point out Greg Marshall to me. Then

we'll decide on the best time and place to talk to him—together."

"Sounds good," Ben agreed.

Corey nodded. "Great. I just have one question."

"What?" Hannah asked.

Corey picked up the Quark Pad. "Do you think I'll get to keep this?"

Smiling, Hannah took the tablet back and put it in her backpack.

"Is that a yes?" Corey asked.

Chapter 14

The next morning at school, Hannah spotted Brittney in the hallway. "Brittney!" she called. Brittney turned, looking slightly annoyed.

Hannah hurried up to her. "Sorry to bother you again, but I was just wondering if you could show me who Greg Marshall is. Do you see him anywhere right now?"

Brittney searched up and down the hallway. "There he is," she said. "Over there. Getting a drink of water."

Hannah glanced in the direction Brittney was looking. At the water fountain, she saw a big guy leaning over to have a drink. He had dark, messy hair—kind of long.

As he stood up, he looked over toward Brittney.

Hannah quickly looked away so he wouldn't see her staring at him. When she looked back, he was gone.

But she'd gotten a good look at him. A big guy who looked like Greg would be hard to miss.

Later that morning Hannah pointed him out to Ben and Corey.

"Just when we thought we went to a small school and knew most people—How did we miss him?" Ben asked.

"No idea," Corey said. "But he's not average height, that's for sure."

Between classes, they tried following Greg, but there was never a good chance to talk to him.

Luckily, they all had the same lunch period.

Looking around the cafeteria, Ben spotted Greg sitting at a table by himself.

"This is perfect," Ben said. "He's alone, so we can talk to him."

"But there are lots of people around, so he won't try anything violent," Corey said. "Probably."

The three friends casually approached Greg. "Mind if we join you?" Hannah asked.

Greg looked a little surprised to have three seventh graders he didn't know join him for lunch, but he shrugged and then gestured to the empty seats around him. Club CSI sat down with their suspect.

For a moment they weren't sure what to say. Then Corey asked, "Did you have Mrs. Ramirez for homeroom last year?"

"Yeah," Greg said. "She was nice."

"Yeah," Corey agreed. "I've got her this year."

"Did Brittney have Mrs. Ramirez for homeroom too?" Hannah asked.

Greg blushed and looked down. "Yeah, she did."

Hannah carefully took the Quark Pad out of her backpack. "Greg, did you give this Quark Pad to Brittney?" she asked gently.

Greg looked stunned. "Where did you get that?"

"Brittney gave it to us," Ben said.

"But it was a present! For her! And I went to a lot of tr—" Greg suddenly stopped talking.

"It was a really nice present, Greg," Hannah said. "Too nice. Her mom won't let her keep it."

"I know," he muttered. "She told me that."

Ben took out an ink pad and a white card. "Greg, would you mind letting us fingerprint you?"

Greg looked nervous. "What? Why?"

"For our forensic science class," Ben answered. That was *sort of* the truth.

"I don't think so," Greg said. He started to gather up his things.

Corey decided to go for it. "Greg, the reason we want your fingerprints is we've got the fingerprints of the person who stole a hundred bucks from our class's school trip fund, and we want to see if your prints match. If you're innocent, you shouldn't mind giving us your fingerprints."

"No way. I don't have to give you my fingerprints!" Greg said vehemently. He stood up from the table and looked around, as if trying to figure out the quickest way out of the cafeteria.

"You're right, Greg, you don't *have* to," Ben said quietly. "But like Corey said, if you don't have anything to hide, then why not just cooperate? And if you did do it, you can't run from it. You must know deep down that you're going to be caught. Everyone knows about the missing money."

Greg just stared at them for a few moments, breathing hard. Nobody said anything.

Then he put his head down on the table and covered it with his arms.

"Okay," he said, his voice a little muffled. "I confess. I took the money."

The three members of Club CSI exchanged a quick look. They'd found the thief! Still, they couldn't help but feel kind of sorry for the guy. He didn't seem tough at all. He actually seemed like a nice kid.

"I just wanted to buy something nice for Brittney," he said. "I've been watching her, trying to figure out what she might really like. I thought maybe a piece of jewelry or clothing or something. Then I heard her talking to one of the kids who has a Quark Pad, saying how much she'd love to have one of those."

It seemed as though Greg had just been waiting to tell someone what he'd done. Now that he'd started confessing, he was telling the whole story.

"I knew I didn't have enough money to buy Brittney a Quark Pad. We don't have much money at home. It's just me and my mom."

"So you decided to steal the money to buy it?" Ben asked.

"Borrow!" Greg insisted. "Not steal the money! I was going to pay it back!"

"Okay, we believe you," Hannah said.

Greg wiped the hair out of his eyes. "I remembered

last year when we raised money for our seventh-grade trip, and Mrs. Ramirez kept all the money in her desk drawer. So I slipped into her room when no one was around."

"How'd you get into the locked drawer?" Ben asked.

Greg looked embarrassed. "Actually, I looked up picking locks on the Internet. It wasn't that hard. All I needed was a screwdriver and a paper clip. The lock was old and loose."

"But what about the padlock on the metal box?" Corey asked.

"Well, I remembered the formula for the combination from Mrs. Ramirez's class last year," he said.

"You remembered that formula for a whole year?" Hannah asked, impressed.

"I'm actually pretty good at math," Greg said. "I like it. Anyway, the numbers on a padlock only go up so high, so there are only so many combinations of three numbers that would solve the formula. I worked them all out and wrote them down ahead of time."

"And when you saw the dial was on 35, you figured maybe that was the last number, and that Mrs. Ramirez had forgotten to spin the dial," Ben said.

Greg looked amazed. "Yeah, that's right! I just looked at my list of numbers to see which set ended with 35. Then I knew the combination."

"And when you opened the box, you saw a fat envelope right on top, so you slipped out a hundred dollars, relocked the box, and stuck it in the drawer," Corey concluded.

"Was there a security camera or something?" Greg asked. "It's like you saw the whole thing."

"No," Hannah said. "If we'd seen the whole thing, it wouldn't have taken us this long to come to you."

Greg let out a big sigh. "It actually kind of feels good to tell someone. Don't worry. I'll turn myself in and take my punishment. And I *will* pay back that money somehow."

Hannah pushed the Quark Pad toward him. "Maybe you could return this and get your money back."

Greg shook his head. "I don't think so." He took the tablet. "At least if I can't go out with Brittney, and I'm going to get in trouble, I'll still have one of these."

Corey looked a little disappointed that the tablet wasn't going to end up being his. But then he patted Greg on the shoulder. "It could be worse.

At least you didn't steal the whole four hundred bucks to buy one of these."

"Four hundred?!" Greg said. "I didn't pay four hundred. I only paid a hundred."

"For a new Quark Pad?" Ben asked, astonished.

"That's impossible!" Corey said.

Greg shrugged. "That's what I paid. Now if you'll excuse me, I'm going to go find Mrs. Ramirez and apologize. And arrange to pay back the money."

He got up and walked off. He wasn't happy, but he actually did feel better than he had in days.

Club CSI watched him go, happy to have solved the crime. But there was something bothering Ben. . . .

Chapter 15

"How could Greg Marshall possibly have gotten a Quark Pad for only a hundred dollars?" Ben asked.

He had called a quick meeting of Club CSI that afternoon after school. It was a beautiful spring day, so they met in the park near the school. They were sitting on the fort in the playground. When he was younger, it had been Corey's favorite thing to climb on. Secretly, he still liked it.

"That is an excellent question," he said, balancing on a rail.

"Why are we still talking about this?" Hannah asked. "We solved the mystery! Greg took the money, and he's going to pay it back. Case closed."

A kid climbed up the side of the fort and passed

right by them on his way to the slide. "Excuse me," he said as he brushed by. Before he slid down the slide, he turned back and shouted, "Aren't you guys kind of big for the playground?"

The three friends ignored the nosy kid.

"Hannah," Corey said, "this is definitely worth talking about."

"Why?" she asked.

"Because maybe *I* could get a Quark Pad for a hundred bucks too," he said.

Hannah moved aside as another kid went barreling by.

"Comin' through," the kid said as he headed for the slide.

"I just don't see what the big deal is," she said.

"That's just the point," Ben said. "A hundred bucks for a Quark Pad is a big deal. A great deal. An unbelievable deal! Right, Corey?"

"Yeah," Corey agreed. "Unbelievable."

"Have you really checked the prices all over town?" Hannah asked.

"Yes," Corey said. "I've never seen one for less than four hundred dollars."

"Well," Hannah said, thinking, "what about the

Internet? Maybe you can get them online for a hundred dollars."

Corey shook his head. "I don't think so," he said. "I've searched and searched, and I've never seen one anywhere close to that price."

"Me either," Ben admitted.

Corey turned to him, surprised. "You want a Quark Pad too?"

"Of course!" Ben said. "They're incredibly cool."

A third kid pushed past Hannah. "Come on," Hannah said. "Let's get off the fort."

"And go where?" Corey asked.

"The swings?" Hannah suggested.

"I don't know," Corey said. "We'd have to get three swings next to one another. And then we'd have to swing together perfectly if we're going to talk. And I'm pretty sure I'd swing higher than you two. I'm kind of a daredevil."

"Let's just walk," Ben said, climbing down from the fort.

The three of them walked toward the edge of the park. "I still don't get why you called a Club CSI meeting to talk about this," Hannah said. "If you guys want to buy Quark Pads, just go ahead and buy them."

"'Just go ahead and buy them,'" Corey mimicked. "Great idea. I'll just use the four hundred dollars I forgot I had in my wallet." He picked up a stick and tossed it at a tree. *Whack!*

"The reason I called the meeting is because the case isn't completely over," Ben explained. "Sure, we know Greg took the money. But he's not telling us the whole truth. He didn't just walk into a store and buy Brittney a Quark Pad for a hundred dollars."

"So what do you want to do?" Hannah asked.

"I think we should talk to Greg again," Ben said. "We could go to his house right now."

Hannah looked at Ben in disbelief. "But we don't even know where he lives!" she protested.

Ben held up a small piece of paper. "Sure we do," he said, smiling. "I've got his address right here."

Hannah snatched the paper out of his hand and read it. It listed a nearby street and an address with an apartment number. "Where did you get this?" she asked.

Ben shrugged. "The Internet may not be any good for finding deals on Quark Pads, but it's great for finding addresses."

The apartment building Greg lived in looked rundown. Some of the windows had sheets instead of curtains. The patches of ground outside were more dirt than grass. The cars parked in back were older models, some of them rusty.

They found apartment 203 and knocked. The curtain in the window next to the door was pulled aside and then the door opened.

"What are you doing here?" Greg asked, looking annoyed. "I told you I was going to admit to taking the money, and I did."

"We were just wondering if we could talk to you about one more thing," Hannah asked uneasily. "We don't mean to bother you."

"Well, you are bothering me," Greg said. He stood there looking at the three seventh graders for a minute. The Club CSI members tried to look as nice and friendly as possible. "Okay," he finally said. "Come on in."

They followed him into the living room of the small apartment. It didn't have much in it, but the furniture and the room itself seemed clean. Greg plopped down on the couch. His hair flopped into his eyes. He pushed it back.

"How'd it go with Mrs. Ramirez?" Corey asked.

Greg shrugged. "Not too bad. She was pretty nice about the whole thing, actually. We went to Principal Inverno together, and it's all settled. I'm going to pay back the money in installments. I'm also going to help out around the principal's office."

"That's good," Hannah said.

"So what's this 'one more thing' you wanted to talk to me about?" Greg asked. "My mom will be home pretty soon, and I haven't told her about this yet, so . . ."

They knew what he meant. Greg wanted them to leave before his mom got home.

"We were wondering where you got the Quark Pad," Ben said.

Greg shifted on the couch. "I told you," he said. "I bought it."

"Where?" Corey asked.

"A store," Greg answered, looking toward the front door.

"Which store?" Hannah asked.

"Um . . . Electronics Superstore," Greg said.

"For a hundred bucks?! No way," Corey objected.

Greg threw up his hands. "What is this? A trial? You guys aren't cops. I don't have to answer your questions."

Hannah sighed. Now it was her turn to look annoyed. "No," she said, "you don't have to answer our questions. But why won't you? All we want to know is where you got the stupid Quark Pad. I really don't see why this is such a big deal."

Greg looked at the floor. "They told me not to talk to anyone about it."

"Who's 'they'?" Corey asked.

"The guys who sold me the Quark Pad," he said.

"Well, we're not going to tell anyone you talked to us," Hannah said. "We promise."

"Who were these guys?" Ben asked.

Greg looked at the front door again. He wanted these three kids out of the apartment before his mom got home. They sure were persistent.

"Nick Ross and Alex Gray," he said.

Corey frowned. He'd heard of Nick and Alex, two eighth graders. From what he'd heard, you didn't want to mess with them. Always getting in trouble. They were held back in grade school and were two of

the oldest kids at Woodlands Junior High.

He looked at Ben and Hannah. He could tell by the looks on their faces that they'd heard of Nick and Alex too.

"Since when do Nick and Alex sell Quark Pads?" Ben asked.

Greg shrugged. "I don't know. But they do. For cheap."

"Thanks for telling us, Greg," Hannah said. "We appreciate it." She stood up, figuring they were done. If the Quark Pad came from Nick Ross and Alex Gray, she didn't want to have anything more to do with it.

But Ben was still sitting down, looking Greg right in the eye. "So tell me, Greg . . . How do we approach Nick and Alex about buying a Quark Pad?"

Chapter 16

As they walked away from the apartment building, Hannah turned toward Ben and said, "I do *not* want to talk to Nick Ross and Alex Gray!"

"Fine," Ben said. "I'll do all the talking."

"Those guys are really scary!" Hannah said.

"She's right, Ben," Corey agreed. "Those guys are pretty scary."

Ben walked on for a few steps, then stopped in the middle of the sidewalk to face Hannah. "You know, you're the one who originally had the idea to start a Club CSI. The 'C' in 'CSI' stands for 'crime.' And sometimes the people involved in crimes are scary."

"Okay, first of all, 'CSI' stands for 'Crime Scene Investigation,'" Hannah said. "I'm interested in

investigating crime scenes. *After* the crime has been committed. When the criminals are gone!"

"Right," Ben said, "but sometimes—"

"And second," Hannah quickly interrupted, "we've already solved this crime! Greg stole the money! Just because you two guys want to buy a Quark Pad for a really cheap price . . ."

"Wait a second," Corey said. "I'd like a cheap Quark Pad, but I really don't want to buy one from Nick and Alex. For one thing, I doubt they offer an extended warranty."

Ben started walking again. "You don't have to come along to meet with Nick and Alex if you're afraid."

Hannah hurried after Ben. So did Corey.

"Afraid?!" Hannah said. "This isn't about being afraid. This is about being sensible."

"Because you're afraid," Ben said.

"Okay," Hannah said. "Maybe I am a little bit afraid of those guys. Did you hear about the time when they set the principal's car on fire?"

"That's just a rumor," Ben said, walking on.

Hannah grabbed Ben by the arm and made him stop walking. "Ben," she said firmly. "Just explain to me exactly why you want to meet with those two . . . Neanderthals."

Ben shifted his backpack from one shoulder to the other. "I think it's important to finish a case once we start it. Yes, we found out who took the money. But he took it for a specific reason—to buy one of these Quark Pads from Nick and Alex. For only one hundred dollars. And that seems really suspicious to me."

"Do you think Nick and Alex are stealing the Quark Pads and then selling them?" Corey asked.

"Maybe," Ben said. "I'm not sure. But it seems as though more and more kids are showing up at school with Quark Pads. And I don't think they all just got great jobs or inherited fortunes or won the lottery."

"Kids can't buy lottery tickets," Corey said. "I tried."

"I bet all those kids talked to Nick and Alex," Ben said. "And lived."

The three friends walked in silence till the end of the block. They stopped. This was where they'd go in different directions to get home. Hannah thought hard for a moment, then came to a conclusion.

"Well," she said, "if you think it's important to talk to Nick and Alex, we'll talk to Nick and Alex.

Together. We started this investigation as Club CSI, and we'll finish it that way."

"Agreed," Corey said. "Although I have a question."

"Which is?" Ben asked.

"Can we talk to Nick and Alex one at a time? They don't have to *both* be there, do they?"

Ben smiled. "Whenever I've seen them, they were together. But if we're lucky enough to catch one of them by himself, that'll be great."

"Okay," Corey said, relieved. He was an athlete, so he could take care of himself. Or at least get away. But when it came to Nick Ross and Alex Gray, together, he felt a little nervous.

"All right then," Hannah said. "See you tomorrow."

The next day in Corey's homeroom, Mrs. Ramirez announced that Club CSI had caught the thief, and the missing money was going to be returned. They'd have enough money for their share of the trip to Washington, DC. The students cheered.

"Who took the money?" Victor asked.

"Because the thief came forward voluntarily, Principal Inverno and I have decided not to release his or her name," Mrs. Ramirez explained.

"But I thought you said Club CSI caught the thief," Victor persisted.

"We did," Corey said. "And he—or she—agreed to turn him- or herself in and repay the money."

"Was it you?" Victor asked accusingly.

Corey started to answer, but then Mrs. Ramirez answered for him. "The thief was not anyone in this class. That's all you need to know."

Corey shot Victor a look of triumph. Victor rolled his eyes and looked away.

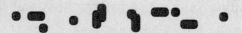

Between classes, Hannah, Ben, and Corey zipped through the halls of the school together, looking for Nick and Alex. They also looked for them at lunch, but didn't see them in the cafeteria.

"Maybe they have a different lunch period," Hannah said.

"Maybe they're busy strangling puppies," Corey said.

"Not funny," she said.

That afternoon they got lucky. They spotted Nick by himself, hanging around one of the water fountains.

"There he is," Corey said. "And I don't see Alex anywhere."

"Perfect," Hannah said. "This is it."

After hesitating for a moment, the three of them walked up to Nick. Ben remembered what Greg had told him to say.

"Hi, Nick," he said. "My name's Ben. I heard you're in the electronics business."

Nick turned his head slowly and stared at them. "Who are you?" he said.

"Ben," he repeated. "And this is Corey and Hannah."

"Where'd you hear I'm in the electronics business?" Nick asked.

"One of your customers told us," Hannah said.

"Which one?" Nick asked.

"He said not to say," Ben answered.

Nick nodded, seeming to be pleased with that answer. "That's right. My customers are all anonymous."

He was leaning against the wall. He pushed himself off and took a step toward the three friends. Corey stood up taller and squared his shoulders. Somehow, with guys like Nick, Corey did that automatically.

"You eighth graders?" Nick asked.

Ben and Hannah looked at each other. What was the right answer? Greg hadn't mentioned this part. They decided to be honest.

"Seventh graders," they declared at the same time.

Nick shook his head. "I don't sell to seventh graders. In my experience, they get excited, and they can't keep their mouths shut." He started to turn away.

Then Corey spoke up. "We'll pay extra," he said. Nick turned back.

"For what?" he asked.

"A Quark Pad," Corey said. "We heard you charge a hundred. But we'll pay you more than that."

"A thousand?" Nick said. All three of them looked shocked. Nick laughed.

"You should see your faces," he said. "Priceless."

Nick rubbed his chin, thinking. Even though he was only an eighth grader, it looked like he needed a shave.

"Tell you what," he said. "I'll sell you one."

The three friends looked relieved.

"That's great," Corey said. "Thanks."

"Yeah, I wasn't finished," Nick continued. "I'll

126

sell you one *if* you follow my instructions exactly."

"We can do that," Ben said.

"Meet me at four thirty today. Come to the park."

"At the fort?" Corey asked.

Nick looked disgusted. "No, not the fort. That's for little kids."

"Right," Corey said. "Not the fort. The swings?"

Nick stared at Corey. Then he said, "You know those big rocks? At the edge of the park?"

"Yeah," Ben said.

"Behind those. Four thirty. Bring a hundred and fifty bucks. Cash."

Before they could say anything about not being able to get together a hundred and fifty dollars in cash by four thirty, Nick turned and then walked away.

Chapter 17

The three friends watched Nick turn the corner of the hallway and walk out of sight. Hannah wheeled on Ben and Corey.

"Where are we gonna get a hundred and fifty dollars in cash?! By four thirty!" she hissed.

"Well," Ben said, "the answer is that I don't actually know."

He started walking briskly down the hall toward their next class. Hannah and Corey followed him.

"Maybe we could borrow it from Mrs. Ramirez's desk," Corey said.

"Very funny," Hannah said.

"How much do each of you have?" Ben asked.

"Maybe thirty bucks," Corey said. "At home, not on me. A little more in the bank. But I can't take it all out. I think there's some kind of minimum you have to leave in there to keep the account open."

"I might be able to scrape together fifty-five," Hannah said. "And then what I've got in my savings account, though I'm not really supposed to touch that. It's for college."

Corey said, "I thought you were going to be a crime scene investigator."

"I am," Hannah said, "but what's that got to do with it?"

"Crime scene investigators don't go to college, do they?" he asked. "They go to the police academy."

Hannah shook her head. "No, they definitely go to college. They get degrees in science before they receive their CSI training. Or at least, *I'm* going to."

"Well, maybe you'll get a scholarship," Ben said. "Because we're going to need your savings. Or at least part of it. I'll get money out of my savings too."

They agreed to run home after school to gather up whatever cash they could find in their rooms. They'd also go to the nearest ATM to withdraw money out of their bank accounts. Together, they were pretty sure they could scrape together a hundred and fifty bucks. Barely.

It was almost four thirty. Ben and Hannah were already impatiently waiting by the fort. Corey came running up.

"Here," he said, handing Ben some cash. "Forty-five dollars. It's all I could manage. And that was with going through my drawers for change."

Ben quickly counted their money. "It's just enough. Let's go." The three of them hurried toward the big rocks at the edge of the park.

When they walked around to the back of the rocks, they saw Nick perched on one of them. On a nearby rock lay his backpack. He didn't seem like the kind of guy who would carry his homework with him at all times.

"Hi, Nick!" Hannah said, trying to keep things friendly.

Nick didn't smile. He lifted his chin less than an inch to show he'd heard her. He jumped down from the rock and slowly walked toward them.

"You bring the money?" he asked, picking up the backpack without looking at it.

"Yeah," Ben said. "A hundred and fifty dollars.

But not all in bills. I hope quarters are okay."

"Did you bring the Quark Pad?" Corey asked.

Nick smacked his own forehead. "Oh, I knew I forgot something!"

The members of Club CSI looked thrown. What were they going to do now? Give Nick the money and just trust him to give them the tablet later?

Then Nick smiled. He pulled a Quark Pad out of the backpack. "Oh no, wait. Here it is."

Behind them, they heard a voice. "What are you doing?!"

They turned and saw Alex Gray walking toward them quickly.

"Oh, great," Hannah muttered.

Alex did not look happy.

"Just making a sale, dude," Nick told him.

"To these dorks?" Alex said, pointing a thumb at Ben, Corey, and Hannah. "What grade are they in?"

Nick shrugged. "I don't know. Uh . . . seventh, I guess."

Alex scowled. "We said no seventh graders. They talk too much."

Ben took a small step toward Alex and Nick. "We won't say anything, Alex."

The big kid stared at Ben. "How do you know my name?"

"Everybody knows who you are," Ben said, hoping to flatter him. "Alex Gray and Nick Ross. You're famous."

It worked. Alex actually smiled a little. "Okay, so you know my name. You're still a seventh grader."

"They said they'd pay extra," Nick explained.

"How much extra?"

"A hundred and fifty."

Alex considered this and then he shook his head. "No," he said with a grunt. "A hundred and seventy-five."

Corey's mouth dropped open. "We don't *have* a hundred and seventy-five!" he cried.

"How much do you have?" Alex asked.

"A hundred and sixty-four," Ben said. He figured Alex really didn't care that much about the money. He just didn't like it that Nick had set this up without talking to him.

"Cash?" Alex asked. Ben nodded. Alex stood there for a minute, staring at him. "Okay," he finally said. "A hundred and sixty-four." He stuck out his hand.

Ben started to give Alex the money. Corey whispered, "Ben! Shouldn't we get the Quark Pad first?"

"It's okay, Corey," Ben said in a normal speaking voice. "I trust Nick and Alex."

Hannah wasn't sure about trusting these two guys doing business behind a pile of rocks in the park, but Ben's tactic worked. Nick and Alex clearly liked being trusted.

Alex took the hundred and sixty-four dollars from Ben, and Nick handed Ben the Quark Pad in a box that looked just like the ones Corey had seen in stores.

"You guys are still getting a really good deal," Nick said. "But keep your mouths shut about this. We don't want all your little seventh-grade friends coming to us."

"Thanks," Hannah said. She offered her hand to shake. Amused, Alex shook it.

"Pleasure doing business with you," he said, grinning.

As the three friends started to leave, Nick said, "Put that box in your backpack. And don't take it out until you get home."

"No refunds," Alex added as he and Nick ran off.

Club CSI went to Ben's room to open the box and check out the Quark Pad. Hannah flopped down in the room's one chair. "I didn't like that warning about no refunds. I hope we're not going to open the box and find it full of rocks."

"It's not full of rocks," Ben assured her.

"How do you know?" Hannah asked.

"It'd be heavier," Corey said. "And it'd rattle. And smell like rocks."

"Just open it," Hannah said.

Ben opened the box and peered inside. Then he reached in and pulled out an electronic tablet.

"Smells like a Quark Pad to me!" Corey said, delighted.

In fact, it looked exactly like the one Greg had given to Brittney. Except that this one didn't have any fingerprints on it—yet.

"Let's fire it up and see what she can do," Ben said.

He turned on the tablet and the screen came to life. They tried out every single app, and they all worked exactly the way they were supposed to. It was a fast, elegant device.

"Well," Ben said. "It doesn't seem like a fake."

"And it doesn't seem used," Corey added. "It looks brand new."

Hannah said, "So it's real and it's new. But is it stolen?"

Ben and Corey exchanged a look. They'd been enjoying trying out the Quark Pad so much that they almost forgot they were investigating how Nick and Alex were able to sell them so cheaply.

"How can we tell?" Corey said. "Look for a sticker that says 'stolen'?"

Hannah used Ben's desktop computer to do a quick Internet search. She found a company website that would tell you if a Quark Pad was registered as stolen. All you had to do was enter the unit's serial number.

Ben found the serial number on the tablet and read it out loud to Hannah. She entered the number into the website and hit enter.

"Stolen," she said.

Chapter 18

After school on Monday, Nick and Alex were hanging out near the parking lot. They hadn't set up any sales in the park. But they didn't want to go home yet. So they were just chilling.

"I gotta say, dude, this is working out great," Nick said.

Alex nodded slowly. "Yeah, it's pretty good."

"Pretty good?" Nick repeated. "It's the most money we ever made! So sweet! And easy, too. The customers come to us, begging to buy the tablets."

Alex nodded. They just sat there, thinking about money.

"What are you gonna do with yours?" Nick asked.

"My what?"

"Your money!"

Alex thought about this. At first, he'd just liked the idea of making the money. Then it was exciting seeing it add up. He'd bought a couple of video games, but mostly he'd just stuffed the money in his sock drawer where his nosy brothers wouldn't find it. He hadn't really thought about what he was going to spend it on.

"I don't know," he said. "Maybe a car."

"You can't drive a car," Nick pointed out.

"Not yet," Alex agreed. "But soon."

"Okay," Nick said. "That's a good idea. Maybe I'll buy a car too."

"No need," Alex said, enjoying himself. "I'll let you borrow my car."

"Thanks, man," Nick said. "Very generous."

Alex made a sweeping gesture across the parking lot. "See any models you like?"

"Nah," Nick said. "Teachers can't afford good cars."

Just as he mentioned the teachers, he noticed that they were starting to come out of the school, heading toward their cars.

"Maybe we should get out of here," Nick said.

"Yeah."

They stood up. Then they noticed three kids

walking toward them. Alex peered at them. "Who is that?"

"I think it's those three dweebs we sold the Quark Pad to the other day," Nick said.

"The seventh graders?" Alex said.

"Yeah."

Alex shook his head. "I told you we shouldn't sell to seventh graders. They're probably coming to whine because they couldn't figure out how to turn the thing on."

Nick and Alex laughed.

Ben, Hannah, and Corey walked up to the two eighth graders.

"I said no refunds," Alex said with a growl.

"We don't want a refund," Hannah said.

"That's good, 'cause you're not getting one," Nick said calmly. "See ya."

Nick and Alex started to walk away.

"Wait!" Corey said.

Alex turned quickly around and put his face close to Corey's. "Look," he said in a low, mean voice, "we told you not to talk about our business transaction. That includes talking to us. Get it?"

Corey didn't back down, even though he felt

nervous. "I get it," he said. "It's just that we want to buy another Quark Pad."

"Another one?" Alex said. "No. One to a customer."

"We're willing to pay more this time," Ben said. "Two hundred."

Alex hesitated. He and Nick exchanged a quick look.

"Two hundred?" Nick asked. "Cash?"

Ben nodded. "We've got it on us."

Alex scratched his jaw. "I don't know if—"

"What's going on here?"

It was Principal Inverno. He'd walked up to the group of five kids in the parking lot without them noticing. Whenever he saw kids hanging out after school, he wanted to know what they were up to. Especially if two of the kids were Nick Ross and Alex Gray.

"Nothing, Principal Inverno," Ben said. "We're just talking."

"Well, school's over for the day," he said. "The teachers are going to be driving through here, so I'd like you to head home. We'll see you tomorrow."

"Okay," Hannah said. "See you tomorrow."

She started to walk away, then turned back. "See you at the rocks!"

It looked as though she were talking to Ben and Corey, but Nick and Alex could hear her too.

"See you there!" Ben said.

"Yeah, at the rocks!" Corey said. "In the park!"

Hannah, Ben, and Corey waited behind the boulders. Hannah drummed her fingers on the rock she was leaning up against.

"I don't think they're coming," she said.

"They'll come," Ben said. "Didn't you see their eyes light up when I said two hundred dollars cash?"

"I kind of wish Principal Inverno hadn't seen us talking to those guys," Corey said. "He might think we're hanging around with them."

Hannah smiled. "We *are* hanging around with them."

"Not really," Corey said. "We're just—"

"Hey, dweebs!"

It was Alex and Nick. They walked up slowly with their hands in their pockets.

"Today's your lucky day," Nick said.

"We talked about it, and we've decided to make an exception to our rule about no repeat customers. We're gonna sell you another Quark Pad," said Alex.

"Two hundred bucks," Nick said. "Cash. But if you go around telling all your little seventh-grade friends, you'll regret it."

"We'll *make* you regret it," Alex threatened.

"Okay, we won't talk about it," Ben said, taking money out of his pocket.

"We'll meet you here tomorrow with the tablet," Alex said.

"Tomorrow," Ben repeated.

"But we need it today!" Corey said.

"Too bad," Alex said. "We don't have one on us right now. You'll get it tomorrow. Of course, if you want to go ahead and give us the money, that's fine."

"Oh no," Hannah said. "No Quark Pad, no money."

"Fine," Nick said, shrugging. "See you tomorrow."

Ben turned to Corey. "I just thought of something. I'll bet Greg would sell us his today. For a hundred and fifty dollars. He could really use the money."

"That's a great idea," Corey said. "Let's go find him."

They started off, but Alex put his hand on Ben's shoulder. "Wait a minute," he said. "Just wait a second."

While Club CSI watched, Alex and Nick stepped away, turned their backs, and talked to each other quietly. Ben, Corey, and Hannah couldn't hear what they were saying, but it was obvious that they soon came to an agreement.

Nick turned back to the three seventh graders. "You want the tablet today? For two hundred bucks?"

"That's what we said," Ben said.

"Okay," Nick said. "Follow us." He turned and started to walk away with Alex.

"Where are we going?" Corey asked.

"To get your Quark Pad," Alex said. "Let's go."

Hannah, Corey, and Ben looked at one another, then followed the two toughs out of the park.

Chapter 19

It was a part of town the three friends hadn't spent much time in.

Or *any* time in, for that matter.

Lots were empty. Buildings were boarded up. Dogs barked behind metal fences.

Nick and Alex just kept walking down the sidewalk. They didn't talk. Corey, Ben, and Hannah followed them, getting more and more nervous.

"Where are we?" Hannah whispered to Ben and Corey.

"I think this is what they call the wrong side of the tracks," Ben answered.

"I don't remember crossing any tracks," Corey said, confused.

"It's just an expression," Ben said.

"I don't like it," Corey said.

They reached a small house with a front porch. The yard was mostly dirt with a few weeds. There was a metal fence around the yard. The windows were covered with boards. It looked as though no one had lived in the house for a long time.

Alex and Nick stopped in front of the house. "This is it," Nick said.

"You live here?" Corey asked.

Alex looked insulted. "No, we don't live in this dump. Why would you think we'd live in a crummy place like this?"

"I don't know," Corey said. "It's a house. You live somewhere. I thought maybe you lived here. Is it more like your clubhouse?"

"'Clubhouse,'" Nick retorted with a sneer. "Little kid stuff."

"Wait here," Alex grumbled. The gate was locked with a chain and a padlock. He put his hand on the fence and started to jump over.

"Shouldn't we come in with you?" Ben asked.

"No, you wait here," Nick said forcefully.

Alex had already vaulted over the fence and into the yard. Nick was about to follow him.

"But if you go in and get the merchandise and then bring it back out here to us, someone might see you," Ben said.

"So?" Nick said.

"Then they'll know where you keep the stuff," Ben pointed out.

Nick hesitated. On the other side of the fence, Alex shook his head, annoyed. "I'm starting to think we shouldn't have brought them here at all."

Nick said, "No one needs to see the merchandise. Give me your backpack. We'll go inside, put the tablet in your backpack, and bring it back out to you. Then you get out of the neighborhood before you look in the backpack."

Now it was Ben's turn to hesitate. "I don't know. . . ."

"How can we be sure you'll put the tablet in the backpack?" Hannah said.

"I thought you trusted us," Nick argued.

Alex threw up his hands. "Come on! Enough talking! I told you seventh graders talk too much. Let's just all go inside. I don't like people seeing us out here with these dorks."

Nick thought about it for a second. He didn't like

to argue with Alex. You never knew what Alex might do. He nodded and jumped the fence. Then he stood in the yard, motioning for Club CSI to come along.

Corey put his hands on the fence and vaulted over easily. Ben managed it, but had to put a foot on top of the fence as he climbed over. The fence rattled.

Hannah stood on the sidewalk.

"Come on, Hannah," Corey said. Nick and Alex were already heading toward the front porch.

"I don't think so," Hannah said.

"What do you mean?" Corey asked. "You can do it."

"Yeah, I can do it, but I don't want to," Hannah said. "I might rip my clothes."

"Come on!" Alex called. "Let's go!"

"I'll just wait for you out here," Hannah said.

"Are you sure that's safe?" Ben asked. "This doesn't seem like the greatest neighborhood."

They could hear a dog barking nearby. Another dog started barking back at the first dog.

"I'll be fine," Hannah said. "Just hurry."

The four boys stood on the porch. Some of the boards were rotted, with gaping holes.

Alex was standing at the front door, spinning the dial on a padlock.

"How come you know the combination to that lock, but we had to jump the fence?" Corey asked.

"Because we put this lock on here, stupid," Alex said. "The gate was already locked when we found this place."

Click. The padlock opened. Alex took it off and hung it on the latch. He opened the front door and went inside. Nick, Ben, and Corey followed him into the house.

Inside it smelled like mildew. There was no furniture, but there were some empty soda cans and fast food bags on the floor.

Corey nudged Ben and whispered, "Look. It *is* their clubhouse."

Alex headed down a hallway. Nick turned and held up his hand. "We'll wait here," he said.

Ben and Corey could see Alex go into a room, probably meant to be a bedroom. Then they heard a click and a creak, as though Alex had opened a closet door.

"You can give me the money now," Nick said, holding out his hand and waggling his fingers.

They heard another sound, like something being pulled down from the ceiling.

"The money?" Ben asked.

"Yeah, the money," Nick said angrily. "You've got it, haven't you?"

"Yeah, I've got it," Ben said. "I just thought I'd pay you when you gave us the Quark Pad."

They heard sounds coming from above the ceiling. Maybe Alex was up in some kind of attic. The house looked small for a full attic, though.

"What happened to trusting us?" Nick asked. "Now, give me that two hundred bucks." He took a step toward Ben.

"Hey, I know what you're doing," Corey said. "You're gonna take our two hundred dollars yourself and then not share it evenly with Alex."

Nick looked like that was the stupidest thing he'd ever heard. "How would I do that? Alex *knows* you're paying two hundred."

"Yeah, but maybe you're gonna tell him we only had a hundred and eighty dollars or something," Ben said. "That way you'll get an extra twenty bucks."

Nick shook his head in disbelief. "He's my partner! I'd never do that. We trust each other. Besides, if Alex found out, he'd kill me. Now give me the two hundred bucks."

As Nick took another step toward Ben, there was a quiet knock at the door. Nick spun around as the door opened.

It was Hannah.

"Hi," she said. "I decided to come in after all. It's kind of creepy out there." She looked around the abandoned house. "Whoa. Creepy in here too."

In the other room, they heard what sounded like someone climbing down and shutting some kind of door. A moment later, Alex came down the hall carrying a box.

"One Quark Pad, coming up!" he said. He pretended to toss the box to Corey, who quickly stuck out his hands to catch it. Alex laughed.

"Okay, now let's have that money," Nick said.

Ben nodded and dug in his pocket. "I'm just curious. Where do you get these Quark Pads?"

Alex smiled a thin, cold grin. "Curiosity killed the cat, buddy."

"Why would we tell you where we got these?" Nick said.

"Did you steal them?" Corey said.

"Shut up," Nick barked. "And give me the two hundred bucks!"

149

Ben handed over the cash. Just as Alex handed him the box with the Quark Pad in it, Hannah put two fingers in her mouth and whistled. Loudly.

The front door banged open. Two cops burst in. "Police!" they yelled. "Stay right where you are!"

Alex and Nick tried to turn and run, but Corey tackled Nick while one of the police officers got Alex. Just as Nick was about to punch Corey, the other police officer grabbed Nick's arm.

"You narcs!" Nick screamed at Club CSI. "You'll pay for this!"

"I don't think so," the first police officer said. "You two are under arrest for selling stolen goods."

Alex sneered. "One stupid Quark Pad. That's nothing."

"There're more tablets," Ben told the police, pointing down the hallway. "Down there, in the bedroom. I think they're hidden up in some kind of attic."

While one police officer stayed with Nick and Alex, the other headed down the hallway.

Chapter 20

Club CSI was meeting with their faculty advisor in the forensics lab the next morning before school. Miss Hodges was beaming.

"I am so proud of you three," she said. "How did you get the police to come at just the right moment?"

Ben smiled. "We arranged all that ahead of time. We talked to Principal Inverno's brother, the police officer."

"He tried to talk us out of it, though," Corey said. "Thought it was too dangerous."

"But we already knew Nick and Alex," Ben said. "We were pretty sure they wouldn't hurt the three of us. They're dishonest, but they're not dangerous."

"I think they would hurt us now, though, if they got the chance," Corey said.

Miss Hodges shook her head. "They won't get

the chance. You won't be seeing those two around Woodlands Junior High anymore."

"Anyway," Ben continued, "we'd planned that Hannah would somehow manage to get off by herself long enough to call the police and tell them where we were."

"That's why I didn't climb the fence and go in with them at first," Hannah explained. "I was calling the police. Then I went inside and whistled when it was time for the police to catch Nick and Alex in the act of selling us stolen goods."

Miss Hodges nodded. "I see. Well, it turns out the whole thing went way beyond Nick and Alex."

"It did?" Corey asked. "What do you mean?"

"Principle Inverno's brother filled us in on everything," she said. "It turns out that Nick and Alex were just the representatives at *this* school. They were recruited to sell the Quark Pads by a big ring of adult thieves. The thieves stole the tablets from the company that makes them, then recruited kids like Nick and Alex to sell them to school kids at a really cheap price."

Corey sighed. "It was such a good price. Too good to be true. And we had to turn in the first

tablet we bought as evidence. I still want one."

"So you're saying that Club CSI helped catch a major ring of thieves?" Hannah asked excitedly. "That's awesome!"

"I sure am," Miss Hodges said. "You should be very proud of yourselves!"

Mrs. Ramirez stuck her head in the door of the lab. "Knock, knock? I figured I might find you here."

"Come in!" Miss Hodges said, smiling warmly at her colleague.

Mrs. Ramirez stepped inside the door, holding something behind her back. "I don't want to interrupt your meeting, but I thought you'd like to know the company that makes Quark Pads is so grateful that they've made a very generous contribution to our school trip fund!"

"That's great!" Ben said.

"Will we be flying to Washington in a luxury jet?" Corey asked.

Mrs. Ramirez laughed. "Not quite. But we might be able to take an extra museum trip or have a special meal while we're there. But they also sent something along specifically for the members of Club CSI. They thought maybe these might help

you with your future investigations."

From behind her back, Mrs. Ramirez revealed . . . three brand-new Quark Pads!

"For us?" Hannah said.

"For free?" Ben said.

"Now *that's* a good price!" Corey said, laughing and reaching for his.

David **Lewman** doesn't remember any funds being stolen when he was in school, but he does fondly remember a class trip to Springfield, Illinois, to learn about Abraham Lincoln. David has written more than sixty-five books starring SpongeBob SquarePants, Jimmy Neutron, the Fairly OddParents, G.I. Joe, the Wild Thornberrys, and other popular characters. He has also written scripts for many acclaimed television shows. David lives in Los Angeles with his wife, Donna, and their dog, Pirkle.

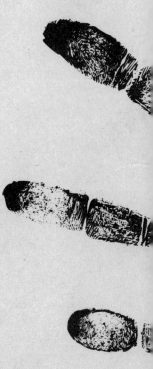

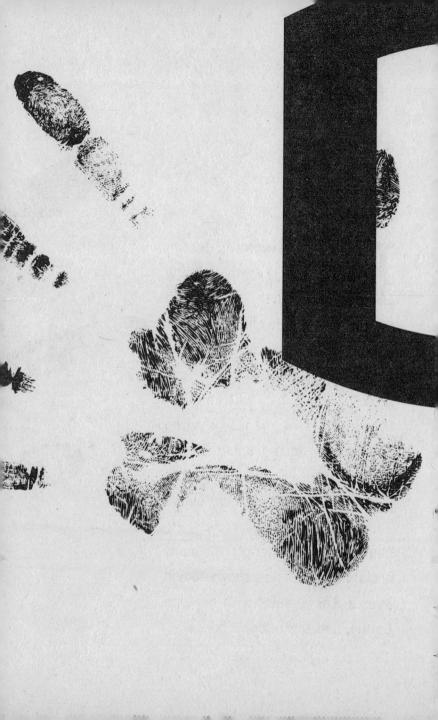